Leo & Henry, August 2020

# CREED: RIDE IT OUT

## A Novel of the Old West

A Creed Nolte Western

Be good to your horse!

T.E. Barrett



T.E. Ba ,

Published by DS Productions
ISBN: 9798654869968

# A READER'S NOTE FROM ROBERT HANLON

This new Western from T.E. Barrett should please those who enjoy the traditional Western novel. Not only is this a well thought out novel—it is a fun read. You'll begin and wonder how you worked your way through it so quickly. In this time of stress, and struggle, it sometimes takes a story like this to put you on the right track, and make your day a bright one.

Read on!

ROBERT HANLON – BESTSELLING AUTHOR OF THE "TIMBER: U.S. MARSHAL" SERIES

# CREED:
# RIDE IT OUT

The dark figure slipped between the rails of the corral. In a soft voice, the man spoke to the horse as he reached out his hand and stepped to his right to block him in the corner.

"Easy, boy," he whispered as he put the rope around the horse's neck, quickly tying a knot and then running his hand under the mane to reassure him. The horse held his head high, worked the air with his nostrils and then sighed to show he was fine. The man led the sorrel thorough the gate. It was dark with no moon, and the starlight threw no shadow. The man tied the horse to a hitching post and went into the barn where he grabbed a saddle, Navajo blanket, saddlebags and bridle. He placed the blanket on the gelding's back, swung the saddle up and pulled the cinch snug. He let the horse stand while he wrote a quick note to his friend.

"Forgive me, but I need your horse and saddle. Here are two twenty dollar gold pieces. I'll explain later." The note was left under the small buckskin bag containing the money. He untied the sorrel from the post, slipped the bridle onto his head, tightened the cinch, fastened the rope on the saddle horn and then stepped into the saddle. The horse jumped slightly to the side just like he thought he might. This was a horse with a lot of spirit, deep in his bones, the kind of horse he needed. The man had just a few hours before daylight and wanted to make the best of the darkness by heading out on a faint trail that led east into the timbered foothills. There was an urgency to blend into the landscape as they rode into the ink of night. He knew he had a price on his head, for he was wanted dead or alive.

As he rode, his mind drifted back to the day's events. He had come to town because the ranch truck needed work, something to do with the carburetor. After he dropped the truck off at the garage, he wandered over to the mercantile to see if there was anything he needed. He casually looked around and then walked out, but that didn't matter, as he was just enjoying the change from his daily work life. He'd been a hired hand at the Rainbow Ranch for four years now, and it was always a treat to get to town for a twenty-five-year-old. He went to the bank for some cash and then stopped off at the Three Dots to get a cold beer. The bartender had all the local gossip, and as he finished his glass, he glanced at the clock and saw it would be a few hours before the truck would be ready, so he thought he'd head on over to his friends, Ben and Nora Ames, for a visit.

There was a warm east wind starting to blow as he wandered down Meadow Road. The dirt road on the edge of town was lined with corrals and small pastures. An occasional gust of wind blew small swirls of dust ahead of him. He grabbed his hat to readjust it on his head as he looked up at the sky. Pure white puffy clouds floated in the late summer's light with patches of pale blue sky showing. The Ameses' house was the last one at the end of the road by the creek that ran through town. Their squeaky yard gate was open and moving back and forth from the breeze. *It's strange that the gate is open*, Creed thought. He stepped onto the porch and saw the front door ajar.

"Hey, Nora, Ben, ya home?" he hollered as he glanced into the opening. There was no answer, so he pushed open the door and stepped inside. In the dimly lit room, Nora was crying, sitting on the sofa.

"Nora, what's wrong?" he asked.

Nora looked up at him, and he noticed that she was looking behind him. He spun as she screamed, "Creed!" just as one of the Spears brothers came at him.

Fred Spears was a big man, more bulky than strong, and his frame blocked the door's light. The smell of liquor on his breath was strong as Creed deflected Fred's right fist that came at him. Creed's eyes had adjusted to the soft light, and he landed a solid right on Fred's chin. Fred staggered back, yelling out his rage. He rushed Creed and grabbed his body with both hands. Creed twisted, getting loose of Fred's drunken grip. Fred was furious as he pulled his hunting knife out of its sheath. Creed met his charge again and pushed him away to his left side, feeling the sweaty heat from his big body.

"Fred, just calm down, drop the knife and let's talk," Creed pleaded.

"The hell with you. I'm going to kill you, you righteous bastard!" Fred yelled as he slashed out with the knife, cutting Creed on the fleshy side of his left hand. Creed watched him like a cat deciding how best to handle a big rat. Fred was two inches taller than Creed at six foot four and weighed forty pounds more at two hundred twenty pounds. The smell of booze was strong, like on some of the stumbling ranch hands on a Saturday night looking for a fight. Fred was different with a totally wild, crazed look in his eyes. This man had been a bully since he was a kid. He was always looking for a fight or for someone to kick around. Creed knew the drink had taken some of the strength and reasoning away from Fred, but he also knew he was dealing with a madman.

"Fred, you've had a lot to drink. Drop the knife and we can talk," Creed said.

Fred kept coming at him, lunging like a man possessed. Creed grabbed the knife arm and twisted it as Fred tried to hit him in the face with his left hand. Creed pushed Fred's right hand up with his left and then landed a solid right into Fred's ribs. The punch stunned him for a second, then Fred blurted out in anger, "You're just like your old man, always butting in!"

"For God's sake, Fred, drop the knife!" Creed begged.

Fred grabbed Creed in a bear hug and pulled Creed off balance as they both got their feet tangled in a throw rug, tripping, falling to the floor with the solid force of gravity. Creed hit the wooden floor hard and felt Fred's body go limp. Creed rolled up onto his side and saw that Fred Spears had the knife deep in his chest.

Creed knelt over him, put his right hand on Fred's neck to feel for a pulse, but there was none. His lifeless eyes stared up at the ceiling. The fresh, warm blood was sticky on Creed's hands and there was a slight iron smell to it as he rose from the floor.

"Oh, my God, he was trying to rape me," Nora cried as she looked on in disbelief. She started to stand but fell back onto the couch. Her short dark hair was a mess, and her blue flowered blouse was off center.

"He and his brothers were drinking at Leo's Bar, and he followed me home as I walked by. I had just closed the door behind me and the next thing I knew he pushed it open, grabbed me, and started slapping me around," she said crying, shaking her head.

"We gotta get the sheriff and get you to Doc Robinson," Creed said.

"I don't need Doc. I'm okay, but you can't go to the sheriff. He's in tight with Old Man Spears and they'd send you to prison, if one of them doesn't kill you first."

"I'll be all right," Creed said as he opened the door wide and stepped out onto the porch with Nora. Just then, the two other Spears brothers came walking down the street, spotting Creed and Nora.

"Creed, you've gotta get out of here. Get out the back. Now! Go!"

Creed was not afraid of a fight, but he knew Nora was right. Just last summer, a local ranch hand had gotten in a fight with Phil Spears at the Three Dots and beat him fair and square. Two days later, the man's body was found in Middle Creek. The sheriff said from drowning, but all those bruises to his face sure made a person wonder. These were bad, evil men and avoiding them was the best thing to do. He also knew he did not want to be locked up in prison for defending his life.

The willows were thick, forming a tangled wall just behind Nora's house. A narrow wooden bridge offered an escape through the willows over the creek and into a hay meadow. Creed stopped at the water, washing the blood from his hands and then quickly wiping them off on his jeans. He stood up and looked behind him. He knew he had to disappear, but where? He had to vanish, that he knew for sure as he ran into the meadow.

"It's not his fault!" Nora screamed as Phil Spears backhanded her and she fell to the floor.

"Get him. Find that son of bitch. Kill him!" Phil yelled at his younger brother, Todd, who stood frozen in total disbelief. Nora lay unconscious on the floor. Phil ran to the back of the house and looked up and down the meadow. He ran back into the house and picked up the phone and turned the crank to get the operator.

"Stella, get the sheriff," he yelled. "Tell him Creed killed my brother, Fred, out at Ben and Nora's place and that he's afoot and should be easy to find. Tell the sheriff to shoot him on sight."

***

The sorrel trotted through the open timber. Creed figured they'd look for him first at the Rainbow. Ben and Nora were his only true friends in town. He'd broken up with his girlfriend about six months prior, and there was no need to stay, since his parents had died in a house fire three years previously in 1932.

In the hours since the incident, he reasoned he now had two important stops to make. The first was to see an old family friend, Rory O'Neill, who lived near the town of Susanville; and the other was a good friend, Bud Jones, who had moved to Jackson, Wyoming and was always inviting him to come "see it for himself." It was a big ride, and he knew he needed help to get to the Rockies from the Sierras.

Traveling horseback at night was something he enjoyed. He had fond memories of riding back to camp after a day's hunt with his dad. It always amazed him how a horse knew how to find its way back in the darkest of nights. He'd just give the horse his head and watch the stars as the horse picked his way back over the trail. The solitude and the quiet pleased him. This time, however, he was on edge. He'd stop every once in a while and look and listen to his back trail.

As dawn's light broke, Creed was near the outskirts of the small town of Taylorsville. He had ridden off the main trail into a small secluded clearing with good grass for the horse. From here, he could get a glimpse of any activity in the little town. For his safety, it was best to avoid people for now and travel at night. He was hungry, thirsty, and physically and emotionally drained.

Creed pulled the saddle and blanket off the horse and then slipped off the bridle. The sorrel's back was dark with sweat. Creed retied the lead rope with a snug bowline knot around the gelding's neck and then tied the other end of it to the top of a young slender pine that gave to the pulls as the horse grazed while Creed tried to get some shut-eye. It was early September. The air was warm with the strong scent of pine as he quickly drifted off.

He had probably slept two hours when he awoke to the noisy squawk of a Steller's jay in the tree above him, and then he heard the sound of horses' metal shoes hitting rocks and of men talking. He scurried from where he had been sleeping and saw five riders coming his way. He quickly reasoned there was nowhere for him to go. He ran to his horse and turned him loose, then grabbed his gear and carried it deep into the timber. He lay on the dry forest floor and watched as the horse grazed towards the main trail.

"Hey, there's Joe's horse," the lead rider yelled as the second man took down his rope from his saddle, built a loop, and threw it, catching the horse. The men rode about, looking for any sign of Creed and then headed for Taylorsville, leading the gelding. He could hear them talking as they rode off. "If he's here, he's afoot now," they laughed.

Creed had to wait 'til night fell and then walk down the rocky trail to catch the sorrel or another horse. He had all afternoon to reflect on the Spears family. The old man was a well-respected leader in the community. He had a huge ranch, owned Sawyer's Bank and was highly regarded in his church. Creed's mom would say, "He's the type who prays with you on Sunday, and then preys on you the rest of the week." He also knew he was not a good man just in the way he treated his horses and cattle. To save expenses, he'd short his animals on their winter feed. Both the horses and cattle had a lot of ribs showing as they shed their winter coats in the spring. He had three sons from three different wives. *Never quite figured how that worked with his religion,* Creed thought, since the old man was a holier-than-thou ornery bastard. The sons were taught the "embolden rule" quite well by their father. They were all hard on their horses and the people they dealt with. Quite a few of their horses had wither sores or were lame for one reason or another. And it seems that the boys got in fights all the time. "They were just flat out bullies," Creed's dad always said.

Creed knew that if he were caught, he'd be lucky to make it to the jail alive. One of the brothers might kill him or one of their hired men would do it to gain fortune from the Spears family. The sheriff was a man to be reckoned with. Several prisoners had been beaten "while trying to escape," and over the years there had been a prisoner or two who had "hanged" himself in his cell. The old man and the sheriff were bad, but the man he feared the most was Phil Spears who was ten years older than him. His nickname was Craw. He was always mad like there something stuck in his craw, so the nickname stuck. Creed and his dad had several run-ins with him over the years. The first one Creed remembered was when he was ten as he and his dad were looking for some friend's missing horses. They rode up to the Spears' ranch and were met by Craw. Asked if he had seen any strange horses on the ranch, Craw replied, "You better pray to God I don't because if I do, I'll shoot them. Nothing's eatin' our grass but our stock."

Another time, Creed and his dad were at a neighbor's branding. Craw was riding a green three-year-old colt that was giving him some trouble while he was roping a calf and the colt bucked him off. In a fit of rage, he started whipping the young horse about the head and neck when Creed's dad walked up and grabbed the quirt out of his hand.

"You don't treat a horse that way."

"I'll treat him any God damn way I please," Craw snapped back.

"Not around me you won't," Creed's dad said as he threw the quirt to the ground. You could see the anger in Craw's eyes. He was smart enough not to cross Creed's dad and they both knew it.

The last encounter had been about a month ago. Creed was in town getting a load of feed with the ranch truck. Phil had parked his truck to block him in. Creed had asked him to please move his truck or he would.

Phil snarled, "What was that?"

Creed replied, "I only say it once."

Phil rushed him and tried to hit him with a tire iron. Creed ducked as it swished by his head. Craw was off balance as Creed punched him on the side of the head, knocking him to the ground. While he lay stunned on the ground, Creed hopped in the truck, moved it and then drove off. Creed heard rumors at the ranch that Phil was looking to get even. Creed knew it was best to avoid them all.

***

When it was finally dark enough, Creed went for his horse. It was as black as the inside of a cow as he walked the worn trail carrying his bridle. The twinkle of yellow lights came from a few of the houses. He spotted the horse corral on the town's edge. The men were in a log cabin near it. Laughter and loud talk radiated from the cabin into the darkness of the night. The horses stood still. Some were dozing where they stood with their heads hung low, but most were just relaxed with the cooler air. He waited for the cabin light to go out. His eyes searched for any movement around the corral in case somebody was waiting with a rifle. He watched for another hour as he enjoyed the cool night air sinking into the warmth of the day. Finally, he decided he had to catch his mount.

He approached the corral slowly using the pines as shields and still watching for any sign of danger. He stepped inside the corral cautiously and walked through the horses, calmly talking to them in a very soft, low voice so they knew he was there and wouldn't offer to spook or kick. He walked up to the sorrel, putting the reins around his neck first and then slipping on the bridle. "Good boy," he said as he fastened the bridle's throatlatch. They made their way to the gate, and he slowly led the horse through it. Walking away from the corral, Creed stayed low in case a bullet came cutting through the night. Once into the trees and out of rifle range, he swung up onto the sorrel's back, loping to where his saddle was. As he rode, he knew he had to be better about being on guard so he didn't lose the horse again or his life.

"No more stupid mistakes," he said to himself as he quickly saddled the gelding and started for Susanville. Time was of the essence, as he had to get to his dad's friend's place as quickly as this horse could reasonably travel. He rode by an old gnarly apple tree, grabbing a couple of apples as he started up an old pack trail. He figured it would be several hours of riding as he urged his horse into a lope. The movement of the horse and the sense of freedom brought a sense of calm to him.

***

The sun's rays were just coming over the distant eastern hills as Susanville came into view. The heat could be felt on his face with sweat already beginning to form on his brow. Out of the hills and another three miles would get him to Rory's place on the southeast outskirts of town. As he rode, a covey of quail took flight in front of the sorrel, and he just trotted along not even offering to spook. Creed knew he had chosen a good horse as they traveled through the dry grass, sage and bitterbrush. He did determine a little history about the sorrel that was likely started as a four-year-old to make sure his bones were strong and when he was broke, he was well fed. He'd seen horses starved down before when they were first started. They were usually weak and easy to break, but once they were back in good flesh, they always had the "buck" in them. This was not the case with this horse. This gelding was strong and trustworthy.

Rory was out in the front yard, splitting firewood with an axe as Creed rode up.

"Hello, Rory," greeted Creed as he sat relaxed in the saddle, his two hands on the saddle horn. "It has been a while."

"Well, by God, it has been. And you've grown into a man since I saw you last. It is good to see you, Creed. Why, it been about three years when I saw you last. You look so much like your dad and you have your mother's smile," Rory said.

Creed swung down from the saddle and both men shook hands. Rory gave him a big pat on the back. "You and your horse had a good ride," Rory said as he looked at the horse's sweat. "I was just getting ready to cook some breakfast, but let's take care of your horse first. I've got a corral on the back of the barn with a tank of water and some shade. Here, just follow me," Rory said as he picked up his axe, over-handed it, and sunk it into a big block of pine. "Got some good meadow hay for your pony, and how about some breakfast for you?" Rory asked.

"Sounds great," Creed answered as he stretched and yawned.

Creed followed Rory as he led the way to the corral next to a dark brown weathered bat-and-board barn. Light was coming through the gaps between the boards from the morning sun accenting small particles floating in the rays. The heat of the late summer sun could already be felt penetrating the building. Loose hay was stacked above in the loft, and Rory climbed the ladder and pitched down enough to feed the sorrel. Outside in the adjacent corral, there was a frisky blue roan running, bucking and tossing his head.

"That there is Jack. Traded an old rifle for him. He's a good one if you handle him right," Rory said, admiring the young horse.

The two watched Jack as he put on a show. "Nice horse." Creed smiled, following the movement of the roan running back and forth along the fence.

"Yep, he's one fine looking animal. He's a great example of nicking. He got the best qualities from both parents. His mom is a beautiful local mare and his daddy's a mustang, runnin' somewhere out in those distant hills. Jack is one tough horse with lots of go in him," Rory said, glancing to the far horizon.

“Yeah, he is nice, and boy, he’s as quick as a cat,” Creed commented.

Creed glanced across the valley to the eastern hills. The country was big, arid and yellow in the morning light. The unknown land of Nevada was waiting for him to ride into.

Creed unsaddled the sorrel and swung the saddle up onto the top rail of the corral. Next he placed the Navajo saddle blanket on the saddle, wet side up. He led the gelding into the corral and ran his hand down the horse’s neck. “You’re a good horse,” he said as he turned him loose.

“Now let’s get some chow for us,” Rory said.

As they walked towards the house, they started talking.

“I heard the news on the radio in town about how they are saying you killed the Spears boy. I don’t believe a word any of those rat thieving bastards say,” Rory said with a look of total disgust in his green eyes.

“Well, hopefully Nora told them what happened,” Creed responded.

“Nora? Hell, Nora’s in a coma! The report said you were attacking her and one of the Spears boys tried to stop you and that’s when you stabbed him in the back and took off running. The moment I heard that bullshit, I knew you would never have done anything that. Your parents would never have raised a son like that,” Rory said, shaking his head.

Creed was in disbelief. “A coma? She was fine when I left. Did the report say how she was doing?”

“Doctors aren’t sure. The report said her nose was broken and they think a rib or two from when she fell. She’d been hit pretty darn hard.” Rory winced.

"Oh, no... That son of a bitch! She was right saying those Spears will do anything to keep their power. Damn them. She is such a sweet person. She has to be all right. I just can't believe they would hurt her," Creed said in shock.

They entered the dark log cabin and Rory got busy throwing a few sticks of wood into his old iron cook stove to keep the fire going. "What we got to do now is get you out of here, away from the Spears and their sheriff. That sheriff is the Spears' personal vicious hound dog. He won't give up 'til he trees you," Rory said as he flipped several pieces of bacon in a cast iron skillet. Rory walked over to open a window by the kitchen table to dissipate the heat. The coffee water was starting to boil. "So what's your plan, Creed?"

"Well, I've got a basic plan. I'm goin' to ride from here to Wyoming. If I travel horseback, I figure I won't be easy to find and when I get to Wyoming, I'll look up Bud Jones. He always said there are plenty of jobs up there and that the country is beautiful. It is just the from here to there on horseback that may be tricky since I don't know the country. And I'm hoping by then the truth will have come out," Creed said.

"That's a big ride," Rory nodded. "Two or three eggs?"

"Three would be great," Creed replied.

"You know, your dad sure was a great friend to me and really saved my life after Laurie died. I was hitting the bottle pretty darn hard and your dad took me in and helped get me right. He was a hell of a good man." Rory smiled at Creed.

"Yeah, he sure was."

"Here you go, Creed. Enjoy," Rory said as he placed the plate on the table.

"Thank you, Rory. I'm starving." As Creed was eating, he told Rory, "That's Joe Adam's horse in your barn. I left him forty bucks for the horse and his gear. If you wouldn't mind, would you tell Joe to take my horse and gear that are at the Rainbow?"

"I'm headed that way next week, so I'd be glad to do that for you. I'm sure Joe understands your predicament since he's had run-ins with those goddamn Spears over the years. You know I've been thinking, Creed, what you're goin' to need is another good horse to help you get to Wyoming. I've ridden the roan a little bit, and he's a good one. He'll make a great packhorse for you, too."

"Oh, Rory, I can't take your horse," Creed objected.

"You're not takin' him. I'm givin' him to you. I want to help you, and as a token of my appreciation of your dad and mom, it would make me feel damn good. After I heard the news, my mind got busy thinking what I would do in your situation. Going horseback makes perfect sense to me, also. Now, I've got just about everything you're gonna need," Rory said as he sat down at the table and started eating his meal.

"Now out in the tack room, I've put a pile of stuff together for you, thinking—actually, hoping—you'd come this way. Now there's an old sawbuck packsaddle, two nice canvas panniers, two good lash ropes for packing and picketing—yep, you can picket Jack by a front leg—and there're two thick canvas manny tarps in the pile, two canvas feedbags, and a sack of oats that I split into two sacks. And there's a canteen, a currycomb, my old .22 rifle with two boxes of shells and some canned meat, beans and cooking oil. And I know it's hotter than blazes right now, but by the time you hit the Rockies, it is gonna be downright chilly, so I gave you a jacket and a sleeping blanket. Oh, and a change of clothes for you. Gosh, I think that is everything." Rory chuckled.

"Thank you so much, Rory. I really appreciate it." Creed smiled warmly.

"You know, I'm half tempted to go with you, but hell, I'd slow you up," Rory said with a big grin.

"Thanks, Rory," Creed said again.

"Don't mention it. It's my pleasure, Creed. You've got to get into Nevada and then I think you got a good chance of making it. You want to avoid them Spears like the plague," Rory said as he pulled a piece of paper out of a drawer and smoothed it out on the table. He drew three large squares for Nevada, Idaho and Wyoming that Creed would be riding into.

"I'm goin' draw you a little bit of a map to help with the trip showing the major roadways, train tracks and rivers. First, I'll draw the two major highways, train tracks and towns. It's one hell of a rough map, but it will give you an idea of the lay of the land. Now," Rory said as he drew on the paper, "you'll leave here and ride near the alkali flats of Honey Lake and into the playa country of the Smoke Creek Desert and then over to Gerlach." Drawing circles for the desert areas, Rory kept explaining, "As the crow flies, it's about thirty-five miles to the Nevada line. Gerlach is your first cluster of buildings you'll ride into. It ain't much. From there, you head for Winnemucca." Rory took a big gulp of coffee and then he wrote down the names as he was explaining. "The Western Pacific has a track that is as good as a map. The tracks head right for Winnemucca and they pretty much parallel the highway to the south. The trains traveling in the distance will help at night with their lights. There's an old wagon road that works its way to

Winnemucca that parallels the tracks from a distance. I've got a great friend in Winnemucca who will help you, and he'll give you directions from there for going into Idaho and Wyoming. If you travel too far to the east, you'll hit the other highway. That one runs north and south. North takes you to Twin Falls. You're goin' to have days of dry camps and some days of short grass for the horses, but you can do it with these two strong horses. But before you get ready, we better put some new shoes on these ponies."

Rory had shod horses for the cavalry with Creed's dad. They both met at Fort Riley, Kansas and worked with the horses at the remount station before returning to California. Both men had shod a lot of horses and they'd even handled some of the rough stock. Creed's dad was known for topping off the broncs. Rory once said, "Your dad could ride anything with hair on it and make it look easy."

Rory had a spot off the barn with a shade tree and a forge, safe from prying eyes. He started the fire and as the coal was burning off its dark, heavy smoke, Creed caught the sorrel. Rory moved right along as Creed held the horse. Rory pulled the worn shoes, then with his nippers trimmed the rock hard frog, trimmed a little of the hard sole with a hoof knife, nippered the walls and then with his rasp leveled and shaped the foot. He forged shoes out of bar stock, using his pritchel to make nail holes.

He lifted the shoes out of the red coals and placed them on the foot, causing a cloud of smoke to rise. He would then go back and finish shaping the shoe on the anvil. When he was satisfied with the fit, he'd tack them on. It was a little bit of a workout since the feet were so dry, but Rory moved with ease. Creed was amazed at how agile Rory was for his age. He moved steadily, not wasting a movement as he picked up the horses' hooves and shod them. There was a slight breeze that offered some relief, but the day was downright hot. Both men were sweating. The sorrel was good to shoe, but the roan had only been shod a few times and was a little impatient.

As Rory was nailing a hind shoe on the roan, he said, "Jack's had some bad treatment down the line. When I first got him, he was plumb spooky and wasn't sure of us human beings. He's settled down a bunch. But there is one thing about this horse that is extremely important to know," Rory said as he set the hind hoof back down and stepped toward Jack's shoulder.

"You just have to be very careful around his hind end. I really have to stress this to you, Creed. Somebody was hard on this pony for one stupid reason or another, and I'm guessing they just tried to break his spirit. You never—and I mean never—want to walk up behind him because he might kick you and kick you hard. It's best to place your hand on his neck or shoulder first, talk to him, and then start down his side, keeping your hand on him the whole time you walk around him and never let go. I know you'll get along with him just fine. Your dad really had a way with horses, and I know you have that same gift."

After shoeing both horses, they headed to the house for something to drink. Sitting in the shade on the front porch, they watched a dented pickup truck drive by the house, slowly checking things over like they were looking for something they had lost. The truck just inched down the dirt road and then eventually it came slowly back by.

"That looks like Sheriff Johnson driving, but don't recognize the passenger. They're a long ways from home. Better keep an eye out for him. Old man Spears has total control over that varmint," Rory said in disgust. The truck slowly disappeared towards town. The rest of the afternoon

Creed and Rory spent talking about the trip while packing the panniers and getting everything ready to go.

Rory noticed the cut on Creed's hand.

"That looks like a nasty cut," Rory said.

"Fred got me with his knife before he fell on it," Creed said. "Still can't believe that happened."

"Yeah, it's a bad deal. I do have some iodine in a bottle in the tack room you can put on that. It'll burn like hell, but it might stop any infection," Rory said.

"Thanks, Rory. I'll give it a go," Creed said.

As the burning sun was setting, Creed was in the barn first graining the horses and then throwing down more hay for them when he saw a man approach the house. Creed moved quietly and quickly toward the side of the house where he could peer in a window. He saw the front door slowly opening as Sheriff Johnson was quietly stepping into the house. Standing in the front room, Rory cocked both hammers back on his 12-gauge shotgun.

"Come right in, Will, and holster that pistol or I'll gut shoot you, you son of a bitch," Rory said.

"I'm after the kid," the sheriff said as he lowered his gun.

"I bet you are. Someone to frame to make old man Spears feel good after losing one of his renegade sons." Rory glared back while keeping his shotgun leveled at him.

"The kid stabbed Fred to death," Will said flatly.

"Creed was just defending himself and if you didn't know it, you know it now. He is an innocent man. You stay away from him or you'll answer to me. Anything happens to me or the kid, my friends know to kill you," Rory said, making a sincere threat.

The sheriff was a middle-aged man, tough for his age. He had a deep scar on his left cheek, a souvenir from one of his many unfair fights in the jailhouse. He had a face that reflected his deep down darkness, eyes that were cold and lifeless. He slowly put his gun back into his holster and started backing out the door.

"I'll find him," he said.

"You heed my warning," Rory said, looking into the sheriff's glare that would have terrified a normal man.

The sheriff slipped out of the house.

Creed stepped into the living room and watched the sheriff drive off in the old truck.

"He's a cold-blooded bastard," Rory said.

"I'm glad you were here to greet him," Creed said.

"We've got to get you out of here tonight before he comes back with more men," Rory said, releasing the hammers on the shotgun and then leaning it back in the corner.

"Better get something to eat and have you ready to get out of here when it gets dark," Rory said. Rory heated some beans, got out some biscuits and a poured a glass of whiskey for them both.

Rory was as excited as a schoolboy getting ready for a big adventure as they ate.

"Now, as you get into Nevada, beware of hot springs that can scald you, even cook your flesh. God, some of those waters are hotter than all get out. You might feel them and get a taste before you let your horses drink. Oh, remember, Gerlach is small, just a couple of buildings so not much night light, but watch for it anyway. And Winnemucca might have lights sparkling in the dark." Rory smiled.

"About your friend in Winnemucca, how do I find him?" Creed asked.

"Oh, Garley Moses, glad you reminded me. There's the main and only road that comes in from the north of town. This road takes you to the only bridge in town crossing the Humboldt River, which is not much more than a trickle this time of year. His house is on the other side of the bridge, the one and only."

It was just getting dusky with a slight crescent moon rising and it was time to vanish. Both horses had a good fill of hay, were brushed and then were saddled.

The packed panniers were placed on Jack, covered with a manny tarp and tied in place with a single diamond hitch.

"I've got one more thing for you, Creed," Rory said, handing a pistol and holster to him. "I almost forgot I had this. It's your dad's old Colt .45 that he lent me years ago."

"Well, I'll be. Dad taught me to shoot with that gun," Creed said as he pulled the pistol from the leather and turned it in his left hand. The blue was still good on the steel and the ivory handle had aged into a light amber color. He spun the cylinder and saw it had six bullets in it. "It's a beautiful gun. It will give me a little more protection then my pocket knife." Creed grinned as he strapped it on.

"Yep, I know your dad would want you to have it. And here's a box of new shells," Rory said as he placed them into Creed's saddlebags.

"Rory, thank you for everything. I'll repay you after I get settled," Creed said.

"Never you mind that. Christmas just came early for you this year. Be safe and watch your back. You're dealing with bushwhackers. Good luck. Remember to just keep your eyes open and trust your instincts," Rory added.

"Thanks, Rory, this really means more than you know to me," Creed said sincerely.

Rory and Creed shook hands, said goodbye, and then Creed stepped up into the saddle, holding on to Jack's lead rope, took a dally, and turned east.

***

Creed trotted the horses through the brush. The lights of Susanville glowed in the distance. This new country he was about to enter was drier and harsher than anything he had ever seen before. He traveled into the wide-open space with miles to go before getting to the distant hills. The darkness gave him needed cover as he joined the night.

The fear of someone with a rifle was a constant worry, but he had no choice. It was a matter of getting while the getting was good. Creed brought the horses down to a walk after a long trot. While Creed was watching the terrain ahead, both horses stopped abruptly with their ears pointing forward. His eyes caught movement ahead of him and then he quickly saw two mule deer bounding off to the south. He could see Honey Lake with its broad alkali flats to the north. The horses moved easily over the level ground. The sorrel was full of life and ready to go. Jack wasn't as sure, traveling at the end of a lead rope. There was a mixed sense of excitement and fear as Creed entered this unknown land. He was headed east towards an area that had a name that intrigued him—the Smoke Creek Desert.

He made the best of the night, traveling many miles before sunrise. The morning sun came up hot in the cloudless sky and the air was still. He stared in wonder at the big expanse of land before him. He thought, *I'm just a speck in this huge dry world.* There was a break in the terrain with a small spring and a few mouthfuls of grass for the horses. He rode into the draw just far enough to give him some cover from searching eyes. All he could tie the horses to were some bushy juniper trees. He pulled the panniers and then the saddles and ran his hands down the horses' backs and sides, checking for any sores. Both were fine. He held onto them while they grazed the small amount of forage that was available. After that, Creed made sure the horses were tied tightly to the junipers because he knew that traveling horses would head for their home range no matter how far they were away from it if they did manage to get loose.

The day was long and the air hot before dusk arrived. The horses' bellies were sucked up tight from lack of a good fill of grass and water. He opened a can of beans for his meal of the day. Creed slipped the feedbags on the horses so they could eat their oats. He was very careful as he moved around Jack. The last thing he needed was to be kicked and injured. He saddled them, packed Jack and rode the sorrel, and headed east towards the Smoke Creek Desert in the fading sunlight. He figured a few hours in the saddle would get them across the Nevada line. Rory had told him about the old wagon trails that came through this country. The old Noble Trail was the one people traveled over in their covered wagons headed for California.

Darkness came with pleasant temperatures. Creed felt a sense of relief as the country opened up in front of him and any trace of roads vanished into the brush.

The riding was easy over the big open expanses, and the country was massive with big barren mountain ranges in the distance. They traveled east through the night and into the Smoke Creek Desert country. He always thought of Nevada as a flat, sandy desert from the stories he had heard as a kid, but he was impressed with the unfolding landscape in front of him. The morning sun greeted them with heat as Creed found a boggy spring and some grass. He unsaddled and picketed the horses by tying the lash ropes to their front left pasterns above the hoof, and the other end to stout live sagebrush. Next, he took one of the manny tarps and made a slight lean-to to block the sun. He walked over to the horses as he ate some hardtack Rory had given him. Next, he checked for rattlers as he spread out the other manny tarp. A few horny toads ran out from under a sage, looked up at him and then darted away. No sign of snakes. He felt good as he placed his blanket on the ground before he lay down to sleep under the tarp. It was warm, but sleep came easily. He was at peace with the surroundings.

The manny tarp's flapping is what woke him as he saw both horses standing still at the ends of the ropes, covered with sweat. All the grass had been eaten where they could reach from their picket ropes. The hot sun was slowing moving down on the western horizon and a hot breeze promised a slow coolness. He was sweaty and his clothes were sticking to him. He took off his silver belly cowboy hat and wiped the sweat from his brow onto his light blue shirtsleeve. He untied the horses and led them to the spring. They managed to drink their fill and that pleased Creed. He took a minute and soaked his inflamed hand in the water. He brushed the horses well and then saddled them. This time it was Jack he'd ride and pack the sorrel. He took the lead rope of the sorrel and swung up and into the saddle. He had ridden about a mile when Jack clapped down on the lead rope with his tail and started crow hopping. Creed undid his dally, let go of the rope and Jack unclamped his tail, dropped the rope and then settled down.

"Easy, Jack, easy," Creed calmly spoke as he swung down from the saddle and ran his hand down the side of Jack's neck several times. "Sorry, I was daydreamin' and not paying attention. I really didn't want to bother you like that." Creed grabbed the lead rope of the sorrel and had him in front of Jack as he stepped back into the saddle. Jack was eyeing the rope that Creed just held on to, without taking a dally. Off they went as the hot bright western sky slowly lost some of its intensity and streaks of pink began infusing the few clouds. Creed thought of his dad's old saying about red skies at nights being a sheepherder's delight. Creed figured it was at least eighty degrees and would more than likely drop into the seventies, which was fine by him. There were big flat desert areas ahead of them like dried lakebeds. As the horses walked, a fine powdery dust accompanied them.

The trio moved through this vast country as darkness overtook the sky, and Creed gazed in amazement at the Milky Way. The night sky exploded in starlight. The beauty of the sky with the outlines of the black hills brought a sense of wonder to him. As a kid, he always enjoyed sleeping out under the stars. This was different, not knowing the country and being somewhat fearful for his safety, but there was also a feeling of jubilation in it all. There was a joyful beauty in all the sparkle and the glitter. For a moment, it seemed like the stars were actually touching the earth, and Creed enjoyed the overall feeling of riding into the glittering starlight. The center of the Milky Way was almost as bright as a moon. The stars twinkled a sense of calmness and of wonder to him. The stars of the galaxy were brilliant in their width, depth and length. Over time, were there as many eyes laid upon the stars as there were stars in the Milky Way, Creed wondered?

As daybreak came, Creed spotted a few buildings with some trees and a person walking between the buildings as he was riding towards them. Overhead, he heard the cry of a red-tailed hawk. The early morning temperature was about seventy-five degrees, and the horses were encrusted in sweat and fine dust. This day promised to be another hot one. He approached the area with caution with his left hand near his pistol. He looked all around as he approached the person.

"Are you working for the Solider Ranch?" the short, grey-bearded man asked. "Heard they got a new rider for their cattle."

Creed guessed the man to be in his mid-fifties. He wore suspenders, keeping up his pants on his stout frame; a torn, long sleeve shirt was draped over a large belly, and a greasy-looking cowboy hat that was more grease than hat covered his bald head.

"Nope. I'm just traveling through, on my way to Winnemucca," Creed answered, sensing things were okay.

"Well, welcome to downtown Gerlach."

"Thanks. Happy to be welcomed." Creed smiled.

"You know, they've made this thing they call a car. It's a tad bit faster than a horse, and hell, with the windows down, you can make it downright breezy as you clip along," the man joshed with a grin.

Creed grinned back and then said, "Yeah, but I can't afford the gasoline."

"Hey, neither can I. So where are you coming from on such a fine warm day?" the man asked.

"Over by Susanville," Creed replied.

"Can I talk you into some breakfast? And old man Miller has a corral and hay for your two horses. Come on and follow me, and I can show you where you can put them," the man offered.

Creed pulled his saddles and turned his horses into the small corral as the man threw them some hay. He swung both saddles up onto the corral rail along with their blankets. An old windmill squeaked, barely moving in the limp, warm breeze, but it pumped a trickle of water into the trough that probably had more algae than water in it.

"I see your horses got the playa treatment from the desert. That damn fine playa dust settles on everything out here when it gets bone dry. Come on, son, let's get us some chow."

Creed followed him, looking around as he walked. They entered the old brown wooden house turned almost black by the sun. Inside a plump, white-haired woman was standing by a hot wood stove. The windows were wide open to let out the heat.

"Oh, by the way, I'm Amos Miller and this here is my wife, Alice," Amos said.

"Dear, he's traveling to Winnemucca and he's takin' the slow, scenic route, goin' horseback so he doesn't miss anything." Amos laughed.

"Pleased to meet you. I'm Creed Nolte," he said, reaching his hand out, shaking both Millers'.

"Well, you're probably more thirsty than hungry," Alice replied with a grin.

"Right now, that's kind of a toss up. But whatever you're cooking sure smells good," Creed replied.

"Hope you like steak and eggs," Alice said as she flipped the beef in the pan.

"If you got enough, that would be great," Creed answered.

"Anybody riding horseback across the desert deserves some food and something to drink," Alice smiled.

As they ate, Creed kept looking out the windows. Amos noticed that but didn't say a word. He did joke about the beautiful views, though.

"It kinda of grows on you, but you don't want to be too old if you're moving here." Amos grinned.

After breakfast, all three walked out to the horses. Both horses had had a good roll, and Creed caught them up one at a time and poured a bucket of trough water on each horse to remove the crusted sweat and dust where the saddles had been. He pushed the excess water off with his cupped hand. The water dripped black.

"You are welcome to sleep in the hay shed by the corral if you like. There's a good bit of shade and that little breeze might take some of the heat away. And just so you know, we don't get many visitors, if that will make you sleep any easier," Amos told Creed.

"Thanks. I'm ready for a little shut-eye," Creed said, looking at the horses.

Creed made a spot in the hay, putting down a manny tarp and his blanket, arranged his denim-lined jacket for his head, and then placed his pistol under the jacket near his left hand. It was hot and he could feel the sweat on his body, but he was tired and he was asleep before he knew it.

***

All of a sudden, there he was, Phil Spears, standing over him with a raised pitchfork. "This is for my brother," he growled as he raised the fork ready to strike.

Creed awoke in a sweaty start. It took him a moment to realize where he was. He caught his breath as he sat up. It was about four in the afternoon when he heard his horses nicker. Old man Miller was throwing them some more hay.

"Trying to get a good fill on them before you take off. Alice has something for you to eat," he said, adding, "If you're hungry, that is."

Creed smelled pie when he walked in the house. Two apple pies were cooling by the window and a cut up chicken was frying while potatoes were boiling.

"Come in, come in." Alice was smiling. "Better have a good meal when you can."

As they were eating, old man Miller chimed in, "Figuring you're traveling at night to stay cool, so it seems like a good time to feed you. It's a dry eighty miles or so from here to Winnemucca. The road that goes by the house here is the old Jungo Road. It's an old wagon road that just a few trucks travel on. It will take you to the mining town of Sulphur—if you want to call it a town, since it just has a few buildings. Then there's the mining town of Jungo, which is not much bigger, but it has a bar if you need to wet your whistle. When you leave here, you gotta go about ten, give or take, miles and you'll see a pile of rocks and there's a little spring close by, but not a lot of water. There might be a little grass, but not much. Depends if the cows got to it. I'm afraid it's just tough country," Amos said.

After the meal, Alice handed Creed a flour sack with some food in it and said, "Just a little something for the trail."

"Thank you, Alice," Creed said.

"I put a small jar of salve in there for the cut on your hand," Alice said.

Creed nodded and mouthed his thanks.

It was downright hot as Creed stepped into the saddle and led Jack out past the Millers, waved and said, "Thanks for everything. Alice, you're a great cook. And Amos, thanks for feeding the horses and the road information."

"Safe travels and good luck," Amos hollered.

The trail was dry, and the dust formed a fine powder cloud as the horses walked out. The sun was lowering in the western sky, but it seemed like the hottest part of the day. It didn't take long before the horses were covered in sweat and the country had sagebrush outnumbering the blades of dry grass. As he looked around, he was missing the greener Sierras.

It was late when he saw the rock pile in the dark. Some thin jackrabbits jumped out onto the trail and hopped away. The water formed a nice shallow cool pool. The sorrel stood still as Creed dismounted. To save water in his canteen, he took a drink first then let the horses have theirs. There was enough so they all had a good drink. His meal was a piece of apple pie as he let the horses graze the easy grass. He took some of the salve and rubbed it on his wound. After that, they walked into the darkness.

The first morning light greeted them with warmth. They had left the faint two-track road and set up camp in a secluded draw. He picketed the horses the best he could and set up his sleeping arrangement. He brushed the horses, talking to them as he did. He checked them over again to make sure there were no saddle or cinch sores.

After he made sure the horses were good, he drifted off to sleep and dreamed of a cool spot in the Sierras he liked. The meadow had stands of white barked aspens on its edge with a deep stream meandering through it. Dark trout were darting for cover under the grassy banks. The shade was cool, helped with a light breeze. It was better to be in the sun. He woke sweaty, not living his dream. The air was hot, the ground dried out, and the horses were wet again from their sweat.

Jack had his ears forward and his neck arched. He was acting bothered. Creed tied the rope around his neck and then undid the lash rope on his pastern. He led him over to a cottonwood and tied him solidly. Next, he did the same to the sorrel. Both horses were now snorty, jumping around, pulling back on their ropes. They both blew that powerful blast of air a horse blows through his expanded nostrils when startled. Then he saw the cause. There on the rocky ridge looking down on them was a stout gray stallion with a small band of mares. The mustang was shaking his head and striking a hoof to the ground in a threatening manner at these intruders into his territory.

"Jack, it looks like some of your relatives have found you." Creed smiled, watching.

Jack and the sorrel both whinnied as they spun around on the end of their ropes.

"Easy, boys," Creed said, hoping they would calm down.

The stallion pawed the ground, turned, lowered his head and charged the mares, herding them over the rise and fading out of sight.

He waited for the horses to calm down and then he grained them. He broke camp, saddled the horses and lifted the panniers onto Jack's sawbuck, covered the load with the manny tarp. A diamond hitch secured his light load and he was off. As he entered the night, he could be anywhere in Nevada except for the night passenger train letting him know he was traveling in the right direction.

As they traveled, they came upon a marker of the stallion's range. There in the sage was a large mound of manure. Stallions will pick a spot and use it over and over again to scent their boundary, and this was the Gray's. The stallion was nowhere to be seen, but Creed had to be alert to the fact to keep his horses safe and with him. If a stallion charged and managed to bite or kick one of the horses, that would render him unrideable. The last thing he needed was to be afoot in the middle of Nevada.

The night air was bearable as they traveled. It was about midnight when they passed Sulphur. Amos was right. Sulphur wasn't much of anything. Later that night, he rode past the few buildings that formed the metropolis of Jungo. It was late and dark, but the bar's light looked like a star. Creed was about a hundred yards away as he looked over at the building. There someone was holding onto a post on the porch trying to light a cigarette. A bright glow lit up a man's face as he struck the match, took a puff, and then stepped back inside. Creed could hear muted voices as they traveled past.

"I hope you're both ready for the bright lights of Winnemucca," he said with a laugh.

Miles past Jungo, he again took the horses up a draw away from the faint road and made camp. There was no water at this camp. The dry climate and dust were starting to bother the cut on his hand. It was getting sore and turning red. He poured some water from the canteen over the cut. The water felt good on his inflamed hand for just a moment then started to throb again. He rubbed more salve into the wound. After the horses had grazed, he tied them to trees with their neck ropes. He did not want to risk having them get entangled in their picket ropes if a stallion attacked them. Creed made sure his gun was handy if he had to fire a shot to scare off the stallion. He tried to sleep but was worried. He felt badly there was no water for the horses. He figured he might try to break camp early, but then he saw a truck driving in the distance. He had to wait.

At dusk, he grained the horses again and brushed them. This night he rode the sorrel in case he had any trouble as he rode into Winnemucca. He wanted the horse that had more saddle time. As they rode towards the road, he saw a train off in the distance. The luxury of fast travel made him daydream for a bit.

"Something nice to drink and eat would be a luxury, boys. I'd like that. And I know you both need a good drink of water."

The night sky had a soft glow off to the east, and he figured he was close to Winnemucca. He would once again use darkness for protection. It was mid-September. It was dark enough as he rode to the northwest edge of town. Headlights showed the comings and going of vehicles as he waited for his chance to cross the bridge undetected. He could see Rory's friend's house on Melarkey Street near the bridge crossing the Humboldt River. The thought of flowing water brought a smile to Creed's face.

The horses' hooves pounded a drumming sound as Creed rode over the stout wooden bridge. He rode to the house where he tied his horses to an old thick cottonwood. He stepped onto the porch and knocked on the door.

"Be right there," a voice hollered. A black and white sheepdog came barked from a back room. Opening the door was a bent over, elderly man with a cane.

"You gotta be Creed!"

"Yes, sir, I am," Creed said over the barking dog as they both shook hands.

"Rye, pipe down, he's a friend. I'm Garley Moses, and I got a letter from Rory explaining everything. This here is Rye, and he's a good dog. He likes being a dog and likes to bark, so I guess he's doing his job."

"Well, he's a fine dog, and I don't mind the barking at all," Creed said as he patted Rye on his side.

"Well, we should get your horses taken care of. The corrals are out back," Garley said as he grabbed his old brown cowboy hat, swept it onto his head and hobbled out the door. He motioned to Creed to go ahead of him since he was walking so slowly.

"Throw them in that one, the big one," Garley said, pointing with his cane to the corral by the barn. "The one next to the mule."

The corrals were built on the edge of the river where cottonwood trees lined the north side. The Humboldt River was running more as a drool of a creek than a river, but it was still moving. The night air was pleasant, but warm. *Comfortable, finally*, Creed thought as he pulled the saddles and blankets from the two geldings.

"Creed, you can put the saddles in the tack room and bring your panniers into the house," Garley said.

Creed grabbed his saddle, the sawbuck and blankets and placed them on racks in the tack room.

When Creed returned to the corral, he turned the pair loose and watched them head right for the water as Garley started talking.

"I understand you're riding to the Wyoming country," Garley said. "Been there about thirty years ago. Why, I cowboyed up there in my younger days, working for an outfit out of Meeteesee one summer, up in the Owl Creek country. Never been to Jackson Hole, though, but I hear it's beautiful, though wintery, country. When I left that Owl Creek range, I rode my horse south across the Red Desert and we caught the train at Rock Springs to get back to Winnemucca."

"Never been to Jackson, either, but I have a good friend who just loves it up there. I'm looking forward to seeing him and the country," Creed said.

"I think you'll like it. It's greener than Nevada. Hell, I think just about anything is." Garley chuckled.

Creed had been eyeing the mule. She was standing in the corral braying as Garley used his cane for support to get over to her. He gave her a quick rub behind her left ear and then ran his hand over her eye to remove some eye crust.

"How do you like having a mule? I've never dealt with one."

"Snowflake here is a sweetheart. You know, a mule is a tad bit different than a horse. I do love horses, but a mule is a pretty unique animal. They're a little smarter than a horse, a little tougher in stamina, won't eat themselves to death if they get into the grain barrel, hooves of iron and they definitely have a mind of their own, but it's how you handle them that makes the difference. You gotta treat them right."

"Yeah, I've heard they can be a little bit on the tricky side," Creed said, watching the mule.

"That they can be. Like a horse, you've got to talk to them and show them respect, but at the same time you don't want them to walk all over you. They really just want to get along with you," Garley replied. He patted Snowflake on her neck and said, "This old girl gives me something to do. We take rides through the sage when it's not too hot. And I can talk to her when Rye gets tired of listening to me palaver."

"Where'd you get her?" Creed asked.

"Got her a while back from the Rocking J. One of their hands had been packing stock salt on her, and he's damn hard on stock, and that's putting it mildly. He's the type of fellow who likes to pound on an animal with a big stout stick, just to get its attention. He is not good with animals. As a matter of fact, he should have another line of work, like selling shoes. Anyway, what I'm gettin' at is a mule does not like to be wronged. A mule is an animal that's really a deep thinker and must have some Irish blood in those veins because they never forget a wrong and are willing to wait forever to make it fair and square."

Garley leaned up against a corral post and continued his tale. "Well, anyway, she was being used in a cow camp north of here, high in the hills and was tired of being pounded on, when one day she did her figuring, added and multiplied and calculated she had just enough lead rope on the picket line to lean out and grab hold of his smelly boot as he walked by. Well, you know it must've been a helluva sight to see. She lunged and got a big mouthful of boot just above his heel at the right time, jerked him to the ground and flung him around like a rag doll." Garley was shaking his cane back and forth. "Why, she shook him into next

Tuesday. They had to pack his busted carcass out of that there cow camp and right into the hospital, boot and all. Never heard if the boot recovered." Garley grinned.

"Joe Turner, he owns the Rocking J, was gonna shoot her and I says to him, I says, 'Joe, there's no need to do that. I'll take her' and there she stands." Garley smiled. "She's actually a very sweet mule that treats you the way you treat her. However, I do have to keep an eye peeled for ol' Flynn, in case he wants to get even with her. But last I heard, he is still at the ranch and has a far away look in his eyes, and I'm just hoping Snowflake shook some of the meanness out of that ornery son of a pup."

Creed just grinned at Garley.

As they turned towards the barn, Garley said, "Creed, please help yourself to the hay in the back of the barn and there are crimped oats in the barrel by the far back wall."

"Thanks, Garley. Can I get Snowflake a jag of hay?"

"Yep, that would be great if you wouldn't mind."

The horses were content to see hay again and started right in, alternating shaking their necks and working their tails between their legs to ward off the bugs as they ate. This night brought a change in the weather. The oppressive heat was getting an infusion of cooler air. Big thunderclouds were finally showing in the western sky. Flashes of distant lightning lit up the night sky.

"Finally, a thunderstorm will break this heat." Garley sighed. "My body has been achy for days. This old body is a hell of a weather barometer, but at least it's good for something. Once it starts to rain, the pain usually goes away." Garley looked up at the clouds and said, "I love the rains this time of year. Oh, it's that smell when the wet hits the dry that I really like. The smell of the sagebrush and the grass when they release their smell to the rain, I find so relaxing. This country is goin' to get some of the moisture it needs."

Garley stopped talking and looked over at Creed. "Oh, you've got to forgive for talking so much. I haven't visited with anybody in a while." Garley smiled.

"No problem, Garley. I know how that can feel."

Creed and Garley entered the house that was lit by kerosene lanterns. The smell reminded Creed of his parents' house. There was another smell, a skillet of bacon and potatoes on the far edge of the cook stove. Garley had it all prepared. It was warm and ready to be served.

"I don't know about you, but I'm gettin' a mite hungry," Garley said as he grabbed two plates from the cupboard. "Got some Bear Hunter potatoes if that will do you," he offered.

"It smells great. Anything's better than another can of beans, I gotta say." Creed smiled as he picked up his plate.

"The horses should be good. They've got hay, water, shelter from the wind and rain, and I'm guessing it will rain about midnight with a good lightning show. I got a spare room for you," Garley said as he started eating.

"Well, I sure do appreciate you letting me and the horses stay. And thank you for grub for all of us," Creed said.

"Why, any friend of Rory's is a friend already as far as I'm concerned. It's a pleasure to have you here," Garley replied.

"Well, it is greatly appreciated." Creed smiled.

As they sat at the small wooden table eating their meal, Garley pulled a folded-up piece of paper out of his shirt pocket and said, "Saw this yesterday and thought you should see it," as he handed it to Creed.

It was a wanted poster. It read:

*Wanted for Murder in California*

*Creed Nolte*
*Height 6'1"*
*180 lbs*
*Auburn hair*
*Brown eyes*
*No scars*
*Considered armed and dangerous. May be traveling horseback.*

*$ 1,000.00 Reward - Dead or Alive*

"That's enough to make any man jumpy with that kind of price on his hide," Garley said.

Creed shook his head. "I didn't realize they'd put such a high price on me, but I'm not surprised. They just want their one-sided justice."

"Yeah, Rory wrote that they are a terrible bunch. He did mention they're a bunch of rat thieving bastards." Garley laughed.

"Well, Rory got that right." Creed smiled half-heartedly.

During dinner, Garley noticed the inflamed cut on Creed's hand and said there was a friend of his, Om Gao, a Chinese man who owned a restaurant downtown and made a lotion that works great on wounds.

"Had a horse cut up pretty bad from barbed wire, and Om mixed up a batch of that stuff and, by golly, it worked wonders," Garley said.

After dinner, Garley told Creed how to get to Om's. It was a short walk over to East Second Street. The easiest way in was down a narrow back alley. The door was bright red with a big golden dragon painted on it.

"Easy to find because it is the only Chinese restaurant in town."

"Thanks for the meal. It sure was a nice change, but before I go, I'm going to do these dishes," Creed offered. Garley didn't refuse. As Creed washed the plates, he asked Garley why he lived in such a dry world.

"I guess it just grows on you. I grew up in Sacramento where it can be hotter than a nun's dream in the summer. I was in my early twenties when I met this good-looking woman who lived here. God, she was a beauty. I was just enamored with her. Gosh, she was just plumb beautiful to look at, so I climbed onto the train in Sacramento and came out here to see her. The romance was more physical than anything and it just faded away, but I got a good ranch job as a cow boss and after all these years, here I am. I just love it when the snow melts off and the spring rains come, and the sagebrush gets that pretty, lush, rich green color. Then spring blends into summer and there you go. Summers and winters can get a little long, but they always give way to the other seasons. You know, you just can't hold onto things like a bad relationship, youth or time. It's best to just let them go," Garley said, momentarily lost in his thoughts.

After a short pause, Garley continued, "Now, you better get over to Om's before it gets too late."

Creed washed his face, ran his wet fingers through his thick hair, pushing it back, and left his silver belly hat hanging on the deer antler hat rack by the back door and started walking. The night was warm but mild with orange lightning flashes in the distance as he stepped into the alley and came upon the bright Golden Dragon door. He knocked and a Chinese woman in a long green silk dress opened it.

"Hello. Garley sent me over to see Om Gao." Creed smiled

"You come, come in. Come. Here you come. Wait right here," she said, pointing to a chair at a large table. "I get Om. Be right back. You wait." She smiled and quickly vanished.

As people were moving in and out of the kitchen, an elderly Chinese man in a dark blue shirt and black pants appeared in the room. His long black hair was streaked with grey and was formed into a big thick braid. He smiled as he walked toward the table.

Creed stood up and shook his hand. "Howdy, I am Creed Nolte."

"Nice to meet you. I am Om Gao."

"Very nice to meet you," Creed replied, and continued, "Garley sent me over." He showed his hand. "He said you have a good ointment for cuts."

"Please seat. I look," Om said, pointing with his outstretched hand to the chair. "Please let me see your hand," Om asked as they sat at the table.

Om took hold of Creed's left hand with both his hands and looked at the cut, rotated Creed's hand and then looked at his palm. All the trail dust, the sun and the dander from brushing the horses had made the wound bright red and clearly infected. Nothing had worked on it.

"You wait here. Be right back," Om said. He turned and spoke in Chinese to a young woman in a yellow silk dress. Then he faced Creed and said, "My daughter will bring you bowl of noodles. Enjoy while I get lotion."

Creed just had just eaten, but he was hungry from being on the trail and the kitchen air smelled inviting. He could handle more food, anytime.

The young lady brought a large bowl of hot steaming noodles to him.

"Thank you so much," Creed said kindly as he took the bowl.

Creed looked around as he ate. The cooks were bent over the hot stove, stirring big steaming pots, others were cutting beef, pork and chicken, while still others were chopping vegetables. The smells were pleasantly overwhelming from his days of trail food. The kitchen was alive with activity as several young oriental women in shiny silk dresses placed orders and carried the hot meals out to the customers. There was a buzz of activity in the air as they all spoke Chinese. The women were passing through a sparkling curtain of large glass beads that separated the kitchen area from the dining area. Creed could get a flash of part of the room as they walked by and could see that it was full of customers, even this late at night.

Om came back to the table and sat down across from him. "You a friend of Garley. He very good man. You good man, your palm tells me." Om handed a small dark blue bottle to Creed and said, "Put this on wound. Will heal fast.

Good on horses, too. Put on at night when you sleep. Just a little, not too much. You say hi to Garley."

"Thank you, Om. I will say hi to Garley. What do I owe you?" Creed asked.

"You friend of Garley, no charge. It my pleasure. Take care of yourself," Om said, bringing both his hands together in front of his chest and slightly bowing.

Creed shook Om's hand, thanked him again, and as he turned to walk out the back door, he suddenly saw the side profile of Craw sitting at one of the tables through the bead curtain. He immediately stepped to the side of the opening and in fractions of a second saw several of Spears' hired hands sitting with him. He quickly headed for the red door and the night. The darkness would still have to be his friend for a while yet. Back at Garley's, he told him about Spears and his men.

"You and your horses need a rest. Sleep here tonight and leave tomorrow night. You will be safe here. We'll keep the horses in the barn out of sight. Rory was careful when he contacted me. Anyway, we've got two of the best guard animals around—Rye and Snowflake."

"Sounds good, Garley. Oh, Om sends his regards."

Garley smiled.

"I'll take Rye out with me and get the horses into the barn," Creed said.

Creed opened the barn door and encouraged the horses into the barn. They could get to water from the Humboldt, as trees hid the path to it. Creed figured they'd be safe and away from searching eyes. They needed a rest and a good fill of feed. Flashes of lightning danced in the western sky.

Just before he turned in, he put the lotion on the wound and placed his gun on the nightstand.

Creed slept through the night and awoke to the smell of Garley flipping sourdough pancakes. He noticed his hand already felt better. The morning air had some coolness to it from last night's rain, and that gave a good feeling to the day.

Garley and Creed spent the day visiting and reminiscing about horses they'd known. They enjoyed some lemonade in the late afternoon as they talked about the trip.

"The best way to go is head north across the bridge and then head directly east. If you go too far north, you'll run into sand dunes, believe it or not, and lots of them. When you get out in that open country, if you're too far south, you'll hit Nevada Highway 18. You want to stay on the north side of the road, riding parallel to it, watching the cars from a safe distance, and you'll eventually see the old mining town of Midas. Then you head north to Tuscarora. From there, you head northeast towards Jackpot. If you get confused, just keep riding east, and you'll run into the main highway going north to Jackpot and then Twin Falls, Idaho. Jackpot ain't much, just a few buildings, but you're close to the Idaho line. Where you want to be is Twin Falls for supplies. After that, it's a cakewalk to get to Jackson. Now, remember, son, if you let your horses roll at the end of the day's ride, it will relax their back muscles and they'll do better by you. A corral is a great stop for the night if you can find one."

"I totally agree with that. It's nice for me to have the horses loose in your barn. It will be a great day for them when I can just turn them out into a pasture," Creed said.

Garley pan-fried some steaks for dinner. The sky grew big thunderheads as they ate. As the night blended out the day, Creed headed out to the barn to feed the horses and Snowflake while calling to Rye to join him. A gusty west wind was blowing, and a few drops of rain were hitting his face as he stepped towards the barn. The rumble of thunder could be heard rolling through the clouds. The horses were running and bucking in their enclosed space. Creed just watched and admired their power. He entered the barn and threw hay into the opposite corner bunks. A heavy downpour of rain started to pound the roof, water streaming off the edges as the horses settled down. This was the first real rain in months. The cool air added new life to the horses. They both looked healthy, fully alert and snorty as they moved to the hay. The moisture and the cooler air felt good to them, as it did to Creed, Rye and Snowflake.

Creed waited for the heavy drenching to stop. Creed thought Snowflake was acting a little strange. She was not eating her hay but braying and running about, kicking out her hind legs. She was agitated. As Creed and Rye turned for the house, they both sensed something was wrong. The back door was open. Rye put his nose to the ground and ran back and forth, growling as he did. Creed walked around to the side and looked through the kitchen window. He saw the sheriff, Will Johnson, standing over Garley who was sitting at the kitchen table. Both were watching the back door. The sheriff had his right hand on his pistol and his left pushing down on Garley's shoulder. Rye growled and ran in and started barking.

"Shut that God damn dog up, or I will," the sheriff commanded, pulling his gun from the holster.

"It's okay, Rye. Calm down, boy. Rye, it'll be okay. Please, you have to be quiet," Garley pleaded.

Rye stared up at the sheriff, growling and baring his teeth. The sheriff stepped sideways to face the dog, and Rye jumped and grabbed hold of Johnson's right pant leg. The sheriff cocked the pistol, pointed the barrel at Rye as Garley pushed the sheriff's arm up, and then like a flash of lightning, the sheriff was hit on the side of the head by Creed's right fist. All those years of haying, milking and feeding cows gave him a powerful punch, and the sheriff dropped like a ton of bricks.

"You all right, Garley?" Creed asked.

"He just waltzed in here liked he owned the joint. I thought you were totally safe, but those bastards know. By God, they know," Garley said, shaking his head in disbelief.

Creed looked up and saw three Chinese men standing by the back door.

"Om has had us watch you for your safety. We'll take care of this man. No hurt, just hold for a while, so you can leave," one said as the others were nodding in agreement. The man who spoke picked up the pistol, slowly released the hammer on the gun, and stuck it in his pant's waistband. The three men picked up the sheriff's limp body and carried him out the door to a black car and then drove off.

It was time to go. The night was coal black. Creed spoke softly to the horses while he saddled them in the darkness of the barn. An owl could be heard hooting in a nearby cottonwood. Creed shook Garley's hand, thanked him for everything, gave Rye a pat, and then he swung up and into the saddle, dallied the lead rope of the roan to keep him close and started off at a brisk walk.

They rode into the night, heading northeast across the bridge and away from town. They climbed up on to the slight rise above town, riding towards the eastern hills, avoiding the sand dunes. After a mile, they were trotting, and since they were warmed up Creed would trot and lope the horses in intervals. They felt good with energy to go. Creed could see the distant highway and the occasional headlights that were few and far between. If someone were looking in the sagebrush tonight for the trio, it would be pure luck to find them. After a steady ride, he figured they had traveled about ten miles when he eased them down to a stop. The horses were sweaty and needed a short rest. He looked at the Big Dipper, found the North Star and picked his course by getting a landmark, a small knob, on the distant horizon. They traveled 'til about six in the morning.

There was a place with good grass, some cottonwoods and a seep of clear water. They were all tired from the ride. Creed pulled the panniers off Jack, then the saddles off both. He watered and picketed them, and had a biscuit and a drink of water. He was sleepy and wrapped his blanket around himself as he leaned against a tree. He heard coyotes yapping far off in the distance. He dozed on and off for a while, looking around, checking for signs of people. The rumble of distant thunder finally woke him from his several-hour sleep. A few magpies were talking in a nearby tree.

The morning sky was getting darker as he broke camp. *A rain would be good to wash away our tracks*, he thought. Creed saddled Jack and packed the sorrel. Once on the move, they traveled slightly northeast through the sage and rabbit brush with Creed checking for any recent tracks of a truck on any of the two-track road they crossed. They ran into a small bunch of Hereford cows with their calves in a creek bottom where they had been enjoying the grass and water. He looked about for cowboys but didn't see anybody riding through the sage. Creed had been in the saddle for a few hours when the sky looked like it couldn't hold any more moisture. The rain would soon start. He found a good flat clearing that could make a nice camp. As he dismounted, a grouse flew out of the sagebrush.

After the horses were tied, he grabbed the .22 and walked into the sage. The distinctive sound of a grouse taking flight caught his ear and as he turned a grouse landed. The bird stretched out his neck as he looked around. Creed brought up the rifle, carefully took aim at the bird's head and pulled the trigger, then watched the grouse's fluttering feathers. He walked over and picked up the bird by its feet, admired it and brought it to his camp.

He brushed the horses while they ate their oats from their feedbags. Then he made a shelter with his manny tarp and stout cottonwood branches to block the soon-to-be arriving rain. There was a breeze of cool air that smelled of rain. The dryness had been taken from the grass and land from the previous storm, so he felt safe to build a fire. He gathered the twig-like ends of the dry undergrowth and sage, broke them into small segments, made a small airy pile of them, placed several larger twigs on top and put a lit match under it all. As the flames grew, he placed larger pieces on top to get a real fire going. As he waited for cooking coals to develop, he skinned the young sage grouse and then he cut up the meat into bite size pieces. When the fire was ready, he put oil in his pan and cooked the meat over the glowing coals. As soon as the pieces were slightly browning in the pan, he dropped them on his tin plate and added a generous shake of salt. Grouse was one of his favorite meals.

Big, cold raindrops hit the ground around him as he finished. The horses turned their butts to the storm and dropped their heads as a wind picked up, pushing their tails between their hind legs in the direction of their heads. The coolness was welcomed as he wrapped himself in his thick blanket. He had not realized how tired he was until then, and he quickly fell asleep for the night.

The morning was gray and chilly with a light west wind. His body felt stiff from the night's sleep. The horses' hair was slightly on end from the temperature change and they were a bit snorty. The cold gave them a physically positive attitude towards their enormous world of sage and distant horizons. Creed always appreciated a horse with energy and spirit to go. He'd rather have his hands full with a lively horse, knowing he had to take a deep seat in the saddle to stay with him.

Autumn was making its presence felt with the days warming into the mid-seventies and the nights hovering around freezing. The grass was getting a little better for the horses, and the grain supply was good since Garley had some to spare. Fuel for cooking and warming fires was always available. The stands of aspen usually had the better grass and wood. The little town of Midas was near, but Creed did not feel safe to ride into it. He rode past the yellow lights of it in the dark. He camped a few miles past it.

The country seemed to open up more and Creed decided to ride during the day.

The horses were good with no sores, and the miles seemed easy. There was some daylight left when he cautiously crossed the highway blacktop that was headed north. It was here he saw the road sign for Tuscarora, twenty-five miles ahead. He'd thought the horses could handle a few more miles, but they needed to rest. He found a meadow bottom with good grass a mile from the road with willows for cover, and there he picketed the horses so they could graze. The sky was clear, and without a cloud cover the night would be cold. He put one manny tarp on the ground, then the horse blankets and then placed the other tarp over his blanket. He rolled his jacket into a pillow. He grained the horses and gave each a good brushing then led them to a small creek where they could get water. After the horses were cared for, he built a small fire and warmed a can of pork and beans.

A hint of frost covered the tarp and ground when he woke. The last stars of the night were fading out of view as he stared straight up into the changing sky from his bedroll. Light of the early morning sun was beginning to intermingle with the retreating darkness of the night sky. It was a gradual morning transition of millennium, a calm start to a beautiful day only interrupted by a faint but soothing song of a singing sparrow. The horses were standing perfectly still, waiting for the first warm rays of the morning sun to touch their hides. The world was at peace. Creed started a morning fire to warm his hands first and then the rest of him. He ate one of his last biscuits from Garley, rolled up his blanket and saddled the horses, packing Jack.

Back in the saddle, he traveled parallel to the road and hoped he was far enough away to be out of rifle range. He cautiously rode into the semi-ghost town of Tuscarora about three in the afternoon. He watched as the cemetery passed by and saw the reminiscence of various mining dreams. He was riding by the few remaining houses when a lady's voice greeted him.

"Hello, there."

“Howdy,” he replied as he turned to his right, looking. There, near a house, was a tall slender woman with long black hair holding a paintbrush and standing on the other side of a freshly painted picket fence. She was wearing a white shirt, blue jeans and boots.

“Where ya traveling?” she asked.

“Headed to Wyoming.”

“So, where are you coming from?” she asked.

“Out of the Sierras.”

“I'm guessing you're at least halfway,” she replied. “I believe I'm a good judge of character, so you are welcome to camp on my porch tonight and join me for dinner.”

“Well, that is very nice of you. That would be great. Is there a safe place I can put my horses?”

“I've got five acres fenced off on the hill there,” Iris said, pointing behind Creed, “and you are welcome to kick them out there. There's a stock tank fed by a spring, so there's plenty of water and even a block of salt they might enjoy,” she offered. “You can leave your outfit here on the porch, and I'll walk up with you to the pasture,” she said, setting the brush down and opening the picket gate. “There's not a lot of grass since it's pretty dry, but there should be enough for them to get.” After a pause, she added, “So, how come you're riding to Jackson?” she asked.

“Well, it's a long story, but I'm going to see a friend I have not seen for a long time,” he responded.

She stuck out her hand. “I'm Iris Sweeney.”

Creed wiped his right hand on his pant leg and reached out for her handshake that was soft but very firm and smiled. “I'm Creed Nolte. Very nice to meet you, Iris.”

Creed, leading his horses, followed Iris up the slight hill through the low sagebrush. "Let me open the gate for you," she said as she undid the gate from the post's top wire loop.

As Creed turned the horses loose, Iris said, "Those are two beautiful horses you have."

"Yes, they are, and they are as tough as they are nice looking. They've been good horses all the way."

"You're the first person to come through here horseback in a while. The last time we had someone traveling through that way was early last summer. A man from the Ruby Valley south of here left his wife. Said there was no love left in the marriage. Gave her the house and all its belongings, and then he saddled his horse, packed his mule and rode off headed for Boise."

Iris was resting one hand on to the top of a fence post and the other on her hip as a breeze blew back her straight hair, exposing her long dangling silver turquoise earrings. In the bright sunlight, her pale green eyes sparkled against her tan skin. *Those are the kind of eyes a man could wander into for a lifetime*, Creed thought.

"Thanks for the pasture. So, if you don't mind me asking, what do you do all the way out here?"

"My husband works for the railroad out of Elko, and I inherited the land here. We both prefer to live here instead of town with all the people. It's nice to be away from the poison gossip. The quiet gives me a chance to enjoy the beauty of nature. I get my inspiration from the changing sky and the color of the land for my art. And," she looked towards her house, "this time of year I can grow a big garden."

As they walked down the hill, Creed noticed a small general store.

"Is it open?" he asked, pointing with his chin.

"Yeah, he mostly sells canned goods, flour and sugar, you know, the basics to get you by. Most people go to Elko once a month and buy their supplies. Mr. Green is the storekeep. He is a strange little fellow who watches over his store like a mother duck. He's never married because he treats the store like a mistress. My husband calls him 'Mr. Quacker' because he's an odd duck, but he does sell needed items." Iris flashed her white smile.

"Well, if he has supplies, his store should be just fine," Creed said.

As they got closer to the house, Iris offered Creed a chance to get clean.

"We have an outdoor shower if you would like to use it. The water temperature should be good from the day's sun. See those black barrels there?" Iris said, pointing to the structure. "They're heated by the day's sun and the water is very hot. There's a line of spring water to give an even temperature. It all makes sense when you see it. My husband has a straight edge razor and a mug of soap for shaving down there. And there is a bar of Ivory. Please go ahead and help yourself."

As they arrived on the porch, Creed said, "That would be great," as he grabbed a change of clothes out of the panniers. He walked through the garden of beans climbing the strings, big leafy potato plants enjoying the warm ground, and all types of lettuce plants growing in the hot sun to get to the shower, which was on the east side of the house. There were the two fifty-five-gallon drums that sat on a wooden structure to support them and high enough for the water's gravity flow. The shower was a three-walled wooden slatted structure with a curtain forming the fourth wall at the opening. The floor was formed with large rocks. Creed looked for snakes before he stepped in, turned on the water, felt of it and got under the warm flow with his clothes on. He lathered his clothes, spun for a rinse and took them off in the spray. He held them under the water for a minute to give them a final rinse and threw them on the west wall of the shower to drip.

While he was enjoying the warm flow of the cleansing water, he noticed the shower curtain open ever so slightly. He instantly thought about his forgotten gun, and then he noticed a big yellow cat rubbing against the shower curtain.

"Hey, Mr. Cat, you don't need to scare me like that," Creed said as he breathed a sigh of relief.

After the shower and a shave, Creed dressed in dry clothes and headed for the house where he threw the wet clothes on the porch rail to dry.

"My, you look a few years younger with a shave," Iris smiled.

"I feel a few years younger with all that trail dust gone." Creed laughed.

Iris was busy preparing the meal and Creed excused himself to head to the store to get supplies. He bought canned goods and some hardtack. Mr. Green was a very unfriendly man. Creed knew he was different from Iris' comment, so he didn't bother to try and make small talk, just paid, thanked him and left.

Iris had prepared a nice meal of steak, bread with butter and a huge salad from her garden. As she brought the meal to the table, Creed was looking at her paintings on the walls.

"I really like the vivid colors that you have captured with your paints in your landscapes."

Iris smiled as she passed the salad bowl to Creed.

"Have you lived in Nevada all your life?" Creed asked.

"I have. Born in Ely, my folks moved to Elko when I was four. I enjoy it for its solitude, and Tuscarora gives me a good balance. I get visitors on and off, but I do have a lot of time to myself." She smiled. "How about you? Where were you born?"

"Born in Tahoe City and raised in Quinsy, north of Tahoe. Both my parents were born there, so that was home," Creed replied. "Dad made a living buying and selling horses and cattle."

"Are your folks still in Quinsy?" Iris asked.

"No, they both died in a house fire three years ago, I'm sorry to say."

"I'm so sorry to hear that," Iris responded.

"Yeah, it was a devastating loss. I can finally cope with it after all these years," Creed replied. He changed the subject and said, "I've been working as a ranch hand."

"Well, I hope you like feeding cows, because where you're going it's long-winter country," Iris said.

"You know, I find that quite pleasant. I really enjoy drivin' a team at a leisurely pace as it gives me a chance to check the cattle over and enjoy the day. But over these last several weeks as I've been riding, I've had a lot of time to think, as you can imagine," Creed said. "I've actually been thinking about going into law."

"When you say law, you mean like being a sheriff?" Iris asked.

"No, even though I have thought about that. I've been thinking of going to law school and becoming a lawyer," Creed replied.

"Where and when?" Iris asked.

"I'm still in the thinking stage, so we'll see."

"Why law?" Iris asked.

"During my life, I've seen a lot of injustice done to various people. I would like to offer them some protection. My mom and I used to talk about it. She would say that it was the only way to fight the rich and powerful who take advantage of people who are just trying to make ends meet," Creed said.

"It's a noble cause. I hope your plans work." Iris smiled.

"Time will tell. First things first, I have to get to Wyoming and then go from there." Creed laughed.

As they finished eating, Mr. Green drove past the house. Iris' first response was, "I really don't know why you are traveling through here, Creed, but I find it very odd that Mr. Green is driving off right now. He never closes the store early unless he's heading to the houses, but that's once a month. I'm guessing he is heading to Elko because that is where the nearest phone is and the sheriff. My intuition tells me you're a good man, so you need to catch up your horses and get the hell out of here before they all come back."

Creed took his napkin and placed it on the table, smiled and thanked Iris for the meal and headed out the door. He filled his two feedbags with oats and as he walked up the hill, he thought of his dad's comment about the power of grain for catching horses. His dad always said, "It's amazing that a big animal will come to a small amount of grain."

Creed whistled from the gate for his horses. The horses lifted their heads from grazing, weighed their options, decided oats were better than dried grass and ran to him and the feedbags. Horses aren't gamblers, but a "grain hand" usually beats a "dried-out grass hand." The only thing that might beat a "grain hand" is a "lush spring grass hand" but the "grain hand" is usually the royal flush in terms of bringing in a loose horse. Creed really knew it was the oats in the bags that brought them and not him, but that was okay.

He tied the lead ropes around their necks, slipped on the bags and talked to them and stroked their necks as they ate. He pulled the bags as they finished, and then led them to the house where he saddled them.

He thanked Iris again for her kindness as he threw a diamond hitch over Jack's load and pushed the wet clothes under the lash rope of the pack to finish their drying. Iris handed him a big bag of carrots from the garden and some muffins, which he stuffed into one of the panniers.

"Your horses will enjoy a treat in their diet, and I hope you like muffins. Ride safely... but ride, ride with the wind. I'm guessing you got about two hours to disappear. Take care of yourself, Creed," Iris said, looking at Creed with admiration.

"Thank you for everything. It was so nice to meet you." With that he grabbed the saddle horn with both hands and swung up into the saddle. "You're a kind, beautiful woman, Iris. Take care," Creed said as he tipped his hat.

He rode about a hundred feet, turned around, waved and then trotted down the hill into the bottom where he loped across the big valley to the distant hills. He traveled northeast through the night, watching for any kind of lights or any movement. Morning light caught him in the middle of nowhere with more hills, more sagebrush and more worry. He stopped high on a hilltop to graze the horses. He cut carrots and added them to their feedbags of oats. "This is from Iris to you both," he said. He enjoyed the muffins as the horses ate.

In the afternoon as he was riding up a draw, he heard the sound of bells. In the mellow autumn light, he saw the sagebrush turn into sheep, a band of a thousand head of ewes and their lambs grazing through the brush.

On the skyline, a man was sitting on his horse surrounded by three sheep dogs. "Hello!" he shouted.

Creed waved and rode towards the man.

"Don't see many riders out here," the bearded man said in a slight accent.

"I detect an accent, so where do you call home?" Creed inquired.

"Mexico City is home. My mother is Basque from northern Spain and my dad is from Mexico City. Kind of funny that here am I in northern Nevada in the middle of America. I think they hired me because of my mother. Her brothers have herded sheep for a lot of the big ranches in this Nevada country. Been working for the Strongs for about a year. I am Mateo Gris."

"Nice to meet you, Mateo. I am Creed Nolte." They shook hands.

"Come, follow me back to my camp," Mateo said as he reined his horse over the top of the hill. The dogs trotted along.

The sorrel and the roan watched the sheep as Creed followed the herder as he rode down to his sheep wagon on the edge a pleasant looking meadow bottom with a corral and a creek running through it. Autumn changing willows covered the creek with their multitude of branches and bright colors. At the corral, the willows had been cut back, giving it an open section of stream with clear sparkly water flowing over the colored rocks of yellow, brown, and green. There was even a shed filled with loose hay for the man's horse and a few jugs or holding pens for any ill sheep.

"I rest here after I make a big circle with sheep. This is my main camp, and the ranch is maybe about forty miles to the east near the main highway. That road goes north into Twin Falls, Idaho and south to Wells," Mateo said.

The late afternoon sky was heating up big clouds that had a slightly different look to those of summer. Mateo offered the corral to Creed's horses, and he gladly accepted it and the hay.

To have the horses free of ropes and the chance to roll and sleep flat on the ground was great, plus flowing water from the creek and meadow hay was an extra relief for Creed. The horses could really relax. The chance to sleep and not worry about the horses was just plain relaxing to him, also. Creed placed two separate mounds of loose hay on the ground for the horses. After eating, they were on their sides, enjoying the warm waning sunlight and then twitching in their sleep on the soft ground.

*They better enjoy it while they can,* Creed thought, because the dark clouds were moving their way. Creed hung his saddles from ropes in the shed to keep them away from mice and porcupines. He didn't want them destroyed by their chewing for the horses' body salt.

By the side of the sheep wagon hung a lamb carcass double wrapped in heavy canvas. Mateo slowly unfolded the wraps and exposed the cool meat. He took a sharp knife and cut into the meat and soon had several pieces on a plate. In the wagon, he stoked the stove's fire with thick willow wood. As he was cooking, he placed a bota bag in the middle of the small table. The meat, sourdough biscuits and a can of green peas were soon ready to eat. By the time the men sat down at the small table to a warm meal, the dark clouds had arrived, spitting rain whipped by strong gusts of wind. As they eat, each took their turn at lifting and squeezing the bota bag for a drink of red wine. The cold rain started to come down in sheets. The comfort of the wagon, the heat from the woodstove and the food were greatly comforting to Creed. Looking out the door window, the horses had their butts to the wind-driven rain and their heads held just above the ground; they were trying to hold on to any body heat they could. The sheepdogs were in the shed for shelter.

After dinner, Mateo lit a kerosene lantern and got out a deck of cards, and as they played, the men talked. Mateo asked Creed where he was coming from. Creed replied the Sierras, and that he was headed to Jackson, Wyoming.

"Did you come through Tuscarora?" Mateo asked.

"I did," Creed answered.

"So you meet the beautiful widow, Iris?" Mateo smiled.

"Iris said she was married and her husband worked in Elko," Creed replied with a startled look on his face.

"I think she say that to keep the men away." Mateo smiled. "Her husband big time gambler and has eye for the ladies, if you can believe that. Been gone for over a year now. He left for Elko one summer day to meet a man in town, and he and his truck never been seen since. Half the people think he run away with a woman. The other half think he had a debt much too big to pay, and that he's buried with his truck in some mineshaft. Iris just seems to be waiting for him."

Creed shook his head. "That is a bizarre story. I'd never guess that. I was amazed how beautiful she was and so nice. What you say is a strange tale."

"One day she will face the truth. Everyone checks on her to make sure she is okay and to admire her beauty. She is very sweet person." Mateo smiled. "Many ranchers and hired hands go out of their way to check on her and, I think, they hope maybe to make her their woman."

Creed just shook his head in disbelief. The discussion changed as they were playing cards. Creed asked questions about the lay of the land and if Mateo had seen any other people riding through the country. He shook his head as they watched snowflakes mixing with the rain.

"The winter is not far off, my friend. Your warm days are few, but they will disappear soon. Sometimes with one big wet snow."

The morning was clear and cool with no trace of snow on the ground. Creed woke at daybreak just as Mateo opened the wagon door. Creed was half asleep as he pulled his gun.

"Relax, mi amigo, it is only me."

"Forgive me, Mateo. I am concerned for my life."

"That is a good thing, my friend." Mateo smiled.

Creed fed his horses and checked them over for any signs of problems. They looked good; the shoes were on tight. It always made him feel good to run his hands over his horses. If there were a problem, he'd feel it or sense it.

There was always a connection with horses for him. Everything felt and looked good as Creed stepped back into the wagon.

"Less than thirty miles and you will be in Idaho. More grass and more water, and you can make good time with your horses. The travel is easy, no mountains to climb," Mateo said. Mateo started cutting bacon from a slab as the fire was heating up the stove. He placed the bacon in a skillet and after a bit, added cut up boiled potatoes. After those were cooked, he fried some eggs and poured two mugs of hot coffee. They sat down at the narrow table and enjoyed their warm breakfast as they looked out on the cold wet ground. Old Man Winter was getting ready to knock at the door of summer.

"The river landmark that awaits you is the Snake with lots of water from the high mountains. There is a high bridge that crosses the Snake River gorge at Twin Falls. You need not cross the river, just use it as boundary. Stay on its right side. It will take you towards Idaho Falls," Mateo said as he picked up his mug of coffee.

"I look forward to seeing the big river."

"It is amazing, my friend. You will see," Mateo said and took a sip of the steaming coffee. "Not only the river, but the canyon is really something to see." Mateo grinned.

"I look forward to seeing all of it," Creed said. "Your story of Iris still amazes me. I can't believe her husband would leave her all alone."

Mateo grinned and raised his eyebrows and shook his head.

After the meal and coffee, they talked as Creed brushed and then saddled his horses. Both men were longing, whether they knew it or not, for human companionship. As

Creed placed the light panniers on the sides of the sorrel, then the top pack on the load covered by the manny tarp, Mateo told him of a feed store just as one enters Twin Falls where he could get more grain for his horses.

Creed took his lash rope and put the end of the rope in the middle of the load with the tail towards the tail of the sorrel. He threw his lash cinch up and over the panniers, reached under the horse's belly grabbing the cinch and attached the rope to the hook of the lash, pulled the rope snug and took one wrap on the hook, then that rope was pulled up so it was parallel with the other rope on top of the load and he twisted the two ropes. The tail rope was pulled up through the twisted rope about a foot. From the top he pulled the rope straight to and then back of the right pannier, went underneath to make a sling, pulled slack to the top and then pulled the rope to the other pannier keeping the rope tight, and then pulled the rope tight on top and tied off the small diamond on top of the load.

"Looks like we're ready to go, Mateo. Now, if you get tired of sheep and sagebrush, come to Jackson and look me up. Or drop me a letter at General Delivery, Jackson Wyoming. Okay?"

"I will do that, my friend. You travel safe and stay on your guard at all times," Mateo said.

They shook hands and Creed dallied the sorrel's lead rope as he swung onto Jack and headed north with a slight lean to the east.

Creed reached the top of the hill above the camp and looked back to see that there was a truck stopping and three men were getting out. Mateo began gesturing to them and pointing in an easterly direction as Creed turned and disappeared over the crest of the hill.

The country began to change as Mateo had said it would with more grass and now with vast views of the distant landscape. Mountains and buttes could be seen to the north. The city of Twin Falls would be easy to spot at night with its glow of lights.

***

After several days, Creed rode into Twin Falls in the early afternoon. This was the largest town he had ridden into. He asked someone out working in his yard where the feed store was.

"Keep riding in the direction you're headed, then get onto Shoshone Street and you'll see the 'Magic Valley Feed' sign," a man said, pointing.

When he found it, Creed tied the horses to some young cottonwoods on the side of the feed store's wooden building. The leaves had turned to bright yellow. He undid the lash rope, pulled the panniers from Jack and loosed both horses' cinches before walking into the store. He opened the weathered front door, hitting a small bell placed there to alert when a customer was entering. In the dimly lit interior, he walked by a stack of workhorse collars, a collection of cinches, a wooden barrel filled with buggy whips, a rack of horseshoes, bags of feed and shelves full of tractor parts. The store had a smell of leather, feed and grease.

"Howdy, can I help you, sir?" from behind the counter came the greeting.

"Hello," Creed replied. "I'm looking for a sack of horse oats."

"Well, we have new oats in. A dollar-seventy-five for an eighty pound bag."

Creed placed two silver dollars on the long wooden countertop. As the man picked each one up, he flipped and grabbed them in mid-air then put them in the till.

"Hey, a friend of yours was here yesterday asking if I'd seen a fellow horseback traveling through," the thin man with wire rim glasses said.

"Did he leave his name, or say where he was headed?" Creed asked.

"Nope. Said he was a friend just traveling through and that he would find you eventually," the man said, scratching his neck.

"What did he look like?" Creed asked.

"Well, he is about your height and build, but with black hair and a little older than you. Looks like he's been outside a lot. He almost looked like an Indian, now that I think about it," the man said. "Nice fellow, very polite... Oh, his hat, one of the nicest black hats I'd ever seen."

Creed looked around as he thought, but no person came to mind, not a clue. It could be anyone, but who would be all the way out here looking for him, except the Spears gang?

"Do you know of a place where I can put my horses up for the night and get a bite to eat?" Creed asked the man.

"The Murphy House is pretty near the last of its kind. They've got a boarding house and a stable. Food's good, and it is a good place for the horses. Nice people, the Murphys. It's kind of out of the way on the edge of town," he replied.

The man followed Creed outside and helped him divide the oats into the old gunny sack he had in his panniers. As Creed was packing the roan, he asked for directions to get to the Murphy place.

"Just head north on this road and then east on Addison about a mile or so, and you'll see it on your left. It's a big old two-story tan house," he said.

"Thanks for your help," Creed said as he stepped up into his saddle. He dallied Jack's lead rope and reined the sorrel onto the dirt road. There were just a few cars and trucks on the roads in town. Creed was please to see several people horseback and also some in horse-pulled wagons. The sky was crystal blue and the air was getting colder. It was the type of day that pleased a body.

*Friend or foe*, Creed pondered as he tied his horses to the rail at the Murphy House. He wore his six-gun under his jacket just in case. He climbed the wooden steps up onto the porch, the weathered wood creaking as he walked. He opened the screen door, then the thick wood door with the leaded glass. Inside there was middle-aged woman sitting at a table, peeling apples.

"Hope you have room for one more, ma'am." Creed smiled as he removed his hat. His face was almost black from all the sun he had ridden through. His forehead was snow white from the hat's shade.

"Well, I hope you like chicken and dumplings, garden salad and peach pie." She smiled as she pushed her short blond hair back out of her face.

"It all sounds great. I have not had pie for a while."

"I'm Melissa Murphy," she said as she stood up.

"Creed Nolte, ma'am. Nice to meet you." They shook hands.

"And is it just you who would be spending the night?"

"Yes, ma'am. Me and my two horses, if you have the availability."

"We have plenty of room for you and your horses. Don't get many coming through a-horseback these days. Where you headed?" Melissa asked.

"Jackson, Wyoming to see a friend."

"It'll take you about a week to get up to Idaho Falls and about three or four days to get to Jackson. Old man Taylor who stays here used to drive the stagecoach turn of the century from here to Idaho Falls. They got to use fresh teams, so of course, they made better time. You'll meet him tonight."

Mrs. Murphy took Creed upstairs and said, "Take your pick."

Creed looked about and then pointed. "I'll take this one overlooking the corral."

"That room really catches the morning sun," she said.

"That'll be good. I like to be able to keep an eye on my horses and wake up early with the sun and start out."

Creed led both horses over to the log barn. The entrance to the barn caught his attention because of the huge antlers over it. The barn was big with the eight stalls and four separate corrals attached to it. There was only one horse there, an old buckskin mare that whinnied when approached. He pulled off the panniers and the saddles and turned the horses into one of the west corrals. They walked out about twenty feet and both lay down and rolled. He put his gear in the tack room and carried his panniers to his room.

It was six o'clock when the dinner bell was rung. Already sitting at the table was John Taylor, the retired stagecoach driver with a big white beard and a friendly smile, an old gambler called Tex, wearing a dandy black vest on his scrawny frame who offered Creed a game of five-card stud after dinner. Creed said he'd think about it. Tex replied, "if it isn't one thing, it's two," and Ma Casey, a little white-haired lady with a high Victorian-collared dress who had a glass of brandy in front of her, "for medicinal purposes," she said. Creed sat at the table where he could watch the front door. Ned Murphy, Melissa's husband and their son, Walter, came through the door taking off their hats.

"Those are mighty fine looking horses in the corral," Ned Murphy said as he walked up to Creed.

"Thanks," Creed replied as he stood up and shook hands with the father and son.

"Those horses are in good shape. They're all muscle with no fat like a lot of horses around town, just not getting the work they need. Y'all look like you've come a few miles. Early in the depression, we had more people show up a-horseback, but that has dropped off. If I had my druthers, I rather be a-horseback. To hell with this advanced civilization of being in a goddamn hurry. More power to you for being brave," Ned said as he sat in his seat.

"Dear, why don't you help yourself?" Melissa was giving her husband the eye.

"Yes, dear, I will quit my rant," he commented as he scooped up some chicken and dumplings and passed the bowl to his son who was just absorbing it all with glee, a stranger on an adventure. Why, for a twelve-year-old, there was no better dinner entertainment.

"I miss those horses. Had a lot of different teams, but I miss them all, they were quite the animals," the old stagecoach driver butted in. "They were strong and had great hearts, and it was always a pleasure to be with them.

They were such beautiful animals and I miss their smells," John Taylor said, then went back to enjoying his meal.

The dinner conversation covered local news, the weather that included the anticipated arrival of snow and a host of other topics. Tex said chances of snow within the week were 4-to-1 odds, if anyone would like to wager.

Creed asked about the antlers over the barn door. "What animal did they belong to?"

"Elk," was the answer.

"I have never seen one or anything like it," Creed responded. "We just have mule deer back home."

"They're amazing when you finally get to see them, or better yet hear them bugle," Ned said.

"Bugle, never heard any of this," Creed replied.

"It is borderline magical," Mr. Taylor replied. "It still amazes me every time I hear it. It is just during the rut in the fall. The bulls challenge each other with their calls, and the winner of the fight gets the cow elk harem."

Heads nodded around the table. "Yeah, it's amazing," everyone agreed.

"Where you're headin', you'll likely see them, but it may be too late to hear them. The breeding season may be finished. But if you never have seen them, it will take your breath away," Ma Casey declared.

"They are big animals. The Indians called horses 'elk dogs' because the elk is the size of a horse and the horse is gentle like a dog. Depends on the dog, I guess. But the body of the elk is big, like that of the horse," Ned said.

The evening was spent talking about traveling to Wyoming. John Taylor told a story about how in his younger days he would haul supplies from Idaho Falls to Jackson on the old wagon trail. He said it was a pull going up and a pain going down. They all said that the Snake River would guide him most of the way. The main thing is to stay east or on the right hand side of the river so you never have to cross it. It's a big river they kept saying. But he would have to cross it once to get to the Teton Pass, though.

Creed thanked everyone for all the information and said his goodbyes because he would be gone in the morning. He was going to square up with the Murphys, but they told him, "No charge. It was our pleasure."

"Thank you so very much," Creed said.

Creed stepped out into the darkness. The stars were just starting to show. His horses were standing in the corral and Creed noticed the manger was full of hay. He smiled, mentally thanking Ned Murphy for the hay. He stroked the horses' necks out of appreciation. They had carried him far. It finally seemed like the end of the trail was achievable.

It was early morning as first light was arriving and the town was quiet. Creed had been invited in for breakfast after he had saddled the horses. Melissa had pancakes, eggs and bacon for him with a hot cup of coffee.

"If you get a chance, drop us a line when you get to Jackson. We're all curious about the rest of your trip. I think you are early enough to beat the heavy snows," Melissa said.

"Yeah, it would be nice to get over the pass before it starts laying it down," Creed said.

As he finished, Melissa handed him a sack with some food in it. She smiled and explained, "So you don't starve."

"Thank you so much for everything. I will drop you a line when I make it to Jackson." With that, Creed gave her a quick hug and headed out the door.

Ned was in the barn as he arrived. He greeted him with an offer to pack the sorrel.

"Ned, thanks again for everything," Creed said.

"It's our pleasure. Wish I would ride up there with you."

"Well, maybe next summer you and Walter can head up there," Creed offered.

"You know, maybe we'll just do that. That's a good thought... Yeah, maybe," Ned pondered. Ned quickly added, "Now, when you leave don't cross the bridge, just enjoy the view and travel on the right side of the river. You may want to avoid Pocatello. It's a bigger city and a little out of your way. Fort Hall is a more direct route and has a good general store for you and your horses."

"Thanks, I appreciate the information," Creed said.

After the sorrel was packed, Creed shook Ned's hand, thanked him again and put his left hand on top of Jack's neck and then put his right hand holding the lead rope on the saddle horn and stepped up and into the saddle.

"See you in Jackson, Ned," Creed smiled.

"Sounds good. See you there." Ned laughed.

Creed rode on the quiet dirt streets of Twin and headed for the Snake. He soon arrived at the Jerome Bridge to get a view of the canyon. There was a thick bunch of scraggly junipers growing about twenty feet from the edge, and that was where Creed tied both horses so he could get a close look at the canyon. He carefully walked up to the edge to take a peek. He slowly moved to the south end of the bridge to get a different view. It was breathtaking with the blue-green Snake River way, way down in the bottom and the rocky outcroppings forming cliff walls on both sides of the canyon that added to its grandeur. *Oh, to be a bird and just fly into that great space*, he thought as he stared at the river far below.

As he walked back to the horses, he thought he saw some movement by the junipers. When he got closer, a man stepped out from behind one of the trees. It was Sheriff Johnson from the Sierras with a pistol in his hand.

"You're a little out of your jurisdiction, aren't you, Sheriff?" Creed asked.

"Never you mind that," Johnson said as he stood near the horses with his pistol pointed squarely at Creed's chest. "Those Chinamen gave me some kind of knockout drops and put me on the bus to Reno, but here I am. You just stand right where you are, Creed. We're taking the bus to Elko and the train back to Truckee, and I'm collecting my reward money from old man Spears for your slippery hide," he said as he started walking behind the sorrel. The roan blocked his way. "Get the hell up, you knot-headed son of a bitch," he barked as he slapped the roan's rump hard with his free hand.

The roan was as quick as greased lightning the way he jumped forward. He planted his front feet solidly and then kicked the sheriff full force with both hinds. Rory knew all along what he was talking about. The sheriff was hurled to the edge of the cliff. He landed hard and tumbled to a stop. Sheriff Johnson was stunned as he stood up and tried to regain his balance. He wobbled, raised his gun slightly, lost his footing and tripped backward, falling over the canyon's edge.

Creed ran to the rim but by the time he got there, the no-good lawman's body was broken on the boulders below. Creed was stunned that everything happened so fast. There was really nothing he could do. The sheriff lay dead on the rocks and to try to get help would draw attention to his escape. The sheriff would bother him no more. Creed gathered his horses and swung into the saddle. He was headed to Wyoming in the morning sun.

He had entered a vast fertile area with hay fields, and in the distance snow-capped mountain ranges stood to the east and far north with buttes interspersed throughout the huge landscape. The world opened up in front of him. He traveled east towards the distant mountain ranges. He'd been told by the old stagecoach driver to head in a northeasterly direction toward the main mountain range and stay parallel to them for days of travel. As Creed rode, he wondered if the sheriff had been the man who had asked for him at the feed store.

The openness of the land in front of him was a nice change from Nevada. The terrain was gentle and the grass and the water better for the horses, just like Mateo had said. The cultivated farmland was a major change with wheat fields and hay being put up. For the time being, he was riding relatively close to the roadway. Men working in the fields would wave as he rode by. It was getting later in the fall and the birds were beginning to flock in large groups. There would be flights of chattering redwing blackbirds and the V formations of Canadian geese with their honking sound overhead. The light of day was getting a muted slant to it and the air was turning colder. Ned had given him an old sweater and neckerchief to help stay warm. The sky was a beautiful clear rich blue. But with the beauty, the thought of snow was entering Creed's mind. He knew it was coming, the calm before the storm. He just hoped it would wait until he arrived in Jackson Hole. Time would tell because the weather had no plans for man or beast.

The terrain varied from open to hilly, but the mountain ranges loomed majestically in the distance. *Freedom*, he thought, *waits on the other side.* Nights were spent in the sagebrush country, and it was a kinder environment than Nevada.

As he rode, his mind wandered back to his girlfriend who he broke up with. Suzy Parker was a pretty young woman who had moved to town about year ago. He had seen her around town on and off for several months. He finally met her at community dance and was intrigued. They would go for rides in the hills and meet in town on rare occasions for a meal. Creed was really getting quite interested in Suzy, but then Phil Spears decided to start courting her. Phil had all the time in the world since he didn't have to work. And Phil could be very charming, Creed remembered.

Phil made it a top priority to get Suzy away from Creed and interested in him. It didn't take long for her to see that Phil was not the man he pretended to be. But by that time, Creed had lost his feeling for Suzy. She wanted to start their relationship again, but he was not sure. Then he had to ride for his life.

Creed made a few camps on the bank of the Snake River when he felt safe and away from any type of ambush. The river was amazing in its size. He had never seen a river so wide and deep. The flow of its currents and eddies mesmerized his thoughts. He could lose himself for a moment as he watched the waters roil with an upward push from the depths. The water seemed to go in all directions as it came to the surface and then swirl out into the current.

Someone told him as he traveled north he would see the American Falls reservoir. He saw the immense body of water, but it was the seagulls flying overhead that caught his attention. Seagulls this far from the ocean? He just shook his head. It seemed hard to believe, especially since he rode through Nevada.

Creed was getting close to Fort Hall. He only had a few miles to ride to get there. Ominous clouds had been filling the western sky since noon. It was always interesting to see the development of a very big storm, Creed thought. The clouds seemed to be pushed upward onto themselves, slowly filling in the wide horizon. A big thick black wall of clouds pushed small lighter-colored finger clouds in front of it, the precursors of the soon arriving wet weather maker. The air was cool and getting colder with a strong, gusty west wind. The sky could not get much darker.

There was no fort left at Fort Hall as Creed rode towards a hitching rail. There was an old general store. He swung down from the saddle and tied the horses to a rail. He started to walk towards the general store and out of the corner of his eye he saw a big wolf-like dog running straight at him. He turned as the dog's mouth reached for his leg and at that same moment an Indian woman yelled and the dog disappeared into the willows not to be seen again.

"That's Lucy's dog, about as mean as a cornered snake. He is usually loose at night watching over the store. You don't want to meet him at night unless you're packing a rifle," the lady yelled.

Creed waved at the woman in thanks as he walked. Stepping into the store there were three elderly Indian men seated around a small table playing cards and speaking in their native tongue. As he walked towards them, a man behind the counter said, "That storm is going to hit soon. If you would like shelter for you and your horses, follow me across the road to my house."

"I'd appreciate that very much," Creed said. He followed the man outside and then led his horses the short distance from the store to an old hand-hewn log cabin built from big cottonwood trees. An old log barn with a sod roof and small corral were beside the cabin.

"You can hang your saddles on those ropes in the barn," the man said.

Creed pulled the saddles and blankets and let the horses loose in the corral. Good clean hay was in a manger. Before he left the corral, he hung up his saddles. He walked to the man's cabin, carrying his two light panniers and blankets. It was about five o'clock in the afternoon, but the darkness from the storm clouds made it look like it was midnight. The temperature was dropping rapidly, and Creed could faintly see his breath. To the west was the rumble of thunder and heavy sheets of rain, possibly mixed with hail. The land was open, but for a few cottonwoods growing along an irrigation ditch. Wind gusts were carrying cold raindrops. It was going to be a drencher.

Inside the cabin, the man lit a kerosene lantern and started a preset fire in a corner fireplace. Creed followed the man into the cabin, leaning forward as he came through the low opening for the doorway. The wind pushed the door into him as he stood up once inside the cabin.

"This is a big storm with lots of water, a good fall rain to wet the ground before the winter snows. Good for next year's grass," the man said.

"Thank you for shelter."

"You are welcome, Creed."

"How do you know my name?" Creed asked, surprised.

"A man stopped by yesterday, said he was a friend and asked if I had seen a man traveling horseback with a packhorse. I'm not a betting man, but we don't get many people coming through horseback these days. Figured it had to be you."

"Did he leave a name?"

"No."

"What did he look like?"

"Like you, but with black hair. Nice fellow with a big black hat."

Creed thought for a moment, not sure who that would be as he shook his head. One thing was for certain, it wasn't the sheriff.

Creed looked around the cabin. There were wood carvings of horses, deer and coyotes. Several had buckskin strips that were beaded and wrapped around them. From a back room stepped a short thin Indian woman in her fifties with white braided hair.

"This is my wife, Kate, and I'm Johnny Fox," he said. They all shook hands.

"It is a pleasure to meet you both. I am Creed Nolte."

The fireplace was throwing out heat as the rains began hitting the roof. A blast of cold air and the low pressure from the storm forced a puff of smoke from the woodstove into the room. It was a pleasant smell adding to a sense of comfort. The horses' heads could be seen in the opening of the barn as they stared out as they took shelter from the storm.

The cabin was being hit with a downpour. Water was pouring off the roof. The air was cold and the windows were steaming up.

"How long have you been on the trail?" Johnny asked.

"Gosh, a little over three weeks... Gee, I guess close to a month now that I think about it." Creed smiled.

"So where are you heading?" asked Johnny.

"Well, I have ridden from the Sierras and headed to Jackson Hole to see a friend," Creed replied.

Kate was starting a fire in the cook stove as she listened.

"Thanks again for shelter for me and my horses. You're right, this storm is a big one. It makes me feel good the horses have cover and hay."

"You are more than welcome. It is good to have your horses taken care of. Not only are they your transportation, but also good friends on a trip like yours. I can still feel the cold from the nights when we've been caught in a wet storm horseback," Johnny said.

Johnny turned and walked in front of the fireplace holding his hands out flat to the fire and then rubbing them.

The lightning had caught up with the thunder, a huge flash and then the loud crack on top of the roof. Creed was glad to be in the cabin and not under his tarp somewhere, getting drenched to the gills. As always, he was glad when his horses could have shelter. It always bothered him to see their bodies shake from a cold rain.

"So, has this always been home?" Creed asked.

"No, we grew up in the Salmon River country near Salmon, Idaho to the northwest of here about two hundred miles. We are Lemhi Shoshone, and that is our homeland. Our people had that beautiful land and the government decided to move us here years ago because of a treaty. This land is okay if you like it flat, dry and dusty, but I miss our beautiful mountain meadows and the icy waters with the big fish that came at the end of the summer. It was good catching the fish and having a great feast. Kate and I were there a few years ago, but it makes us sad to have all our people gone."

"Let's eat," Kate announced. She placed steaks and biscuits on the table. The rain was a steady cold downpour and the darkness was now more than the cloud cover.

The food and the warmth of the fire made for a cozy evening. The howling winds slapped the rain against the cabin's logs. Hail hit the windowpanes at times as the wind gusted.

After dinner, they sat around the fire. Kate had poured three big mugs of coffee. As Johnny was holding his mug with both hands, he started talking about the ride.

"Your horses will like the last leg of your journey. There is sagebrush country that a fire burned through a couple of years ago, so the sage is thinned out and there is more grass. The country is flat for the most part but for rolling, gentle hills. You do have to cross the Snake near Victor. There is a bridge that you can cross or a ford up the river about a mile. "

Kate had gotten up and returned from the kitchen with a plate of cookies.

"You will like the country from here to Jackson. You'll have the big mountains in front of you," she said as she sat.

Johnny continued as he glanced into the darkness through the steamed window, "Your horses will have to work to get to the top of the pass, but it's not a bad climb. They might be pushing snow ahead of their chests for a ways, but it's usually a light, dry snow this time of year. From the top you'll see loaves of hay put up by the beaver slides in the hay meadows. It is quite a pleasing view."

"I am really looking forward to it. It will be nice to finally see it and reach my friend," Creed said.

As the conversation ended, Johnny threw a few good pieces of wood on the fire.

"We don't have a bed to offer but there is the couch for sleep," Kate said.

"The couch will be good." Creed smiled.

Johnny and Kate wished him a good night.

Creed lay down to sleep covered with his blanket. The flickering of the flames from the fire caused shadows to dance on the walls highlighting the carved animals. He listened to the rain and drifted off to relaxing sleep.

The morning sky was clear, the air icy and the soil saturated. A dense fog hugged the ground and there was a trace of snow on the grass. The house was warm from the cook stove with a hot pot of coffee steaming. Johnny had been up since daybreak as had Creed who entered the cabin after feeding his horses, and the warmth felt good.

"The horses will like this day. They will travel with ease in the cool. You have a while to get into Wyoming before the cold maker shows up, but he is coming soon. The number of geese flying south is more and more. Head for Shelly by following the road or the river. The town of Shelly about ten miles this side of the Idaho Falls," Johnny said.

"Well, that will be good. I am excited that I am finally getting close," Creed said.

"Creed, I must tell you... I had a dream last night that two men are looking for you, one good and one bad. The good man was in the light, the other man in the shadows. Don't let the man in the dark grab your life," Johnny said, grabbing at the air in front of him like he was trying to catch a flying insect. "You have to be aware of your surroundings and your horses. Keep them close, very close to you."

Johnny took hold of Creed's forearms and started chanting, the chanting lasting about a minute. When he stopped, he told Creed that he gave him a blessing for protection. "It is a warrior's blessing to make you alert and to have good judgment in battle. Be safe, my friend, and watch your horses for warning signs."

Creed thanked Kate and Johnny for their kindness to him and his horses. The soil by the old fort site was slippery for the horses from last night's heavy rain. Later, riding through the cottonwoods by the river's rocky surface, he heard that hollow sound a loose horseshoe makes when it hits a rock. It's a sound that takes a rider a lot of miles to recognize. But once you put two and two together, you know your horse can throw it at any time. Creed knew it the second he heard it. He had to get that taken care of.

The autumn sun still had power and was warming the air. The ground fog had disappeared, giving way to a brilliant blue sky that matched the blue of the Snake River flowing with all of its power. As Creed rode out of the cottonwoods, he could see the small town of Shelley and a blacksmith's shop.

Creed rode up to the big open door and a man wearing chaps stepped out. Creed explained he was traveling to Jackson and that one of the horses had a loose shoe.

The man was built like he was made for shoeing horses. He was compact, about five feet six inches tall, barrel-chested, powerful arms and an easy manner. He was a man who didn't ask questions.

"Those are mighty fine looking horses you got there. There's not an ounce of fat on them. I sure like that roan horse you got. Always been kind of partial to that color," he said.

"Thanks. Couldn't ask for two better horses." Creed smiled.

"It is only the sorrel that needs to be reshod. The roan's shoes should be good enough to make the rest of the trip," Creed explained.

"Those light-colored feet on the red horse aren't as tough as those hard feet on the roan," the blacksmith commented. "I'll tell you what. I'll reset the shoes on both if you split that pile of wood and stack it in the shed for me while I'm shoeing."

"That sounds more than fair," Creed said as he unpacked Jack's load and pulled the saddles off both horses. "You have to be careful with the roan's hind feet. You always have to touch him on his side and back and then run your hand down his leg or he might kick. You don't want to surprise him by just grabbing a foot. He's not a mean horse, but somebody treated him badly before I got him."

"Oh, I have a few that come in here from time to time like that. I think we'll get along just fine."

Creed was close by, splitting the wood, as the blacksmith was working and could see and hear him. As he was swinging the double bit axe, the blacksmith starting telling him a story about a blue roan horse his dad rode as a young ranch hand.

"Pa worked for a big outfit up by the Montana border near Monida, and they had this big beautiful blue roan horse that nobody would ride. The horse would rear up and jump away from you when you went to get on him, and if you did get in the saddle, he'd just want to take off with you. None of the hands wanted anything to do with that horse. Pa said he just looked like too good of a horse to pass up, so he added him to his string. There was a lot of snow that early spring when he started riding him, and he figured those big drifts would take a little wind out of his sails." The blacksmith paused as he pulled a shoe and took his hoof knife to start trimming the sole and frog.

"Pa couldn't just swing into the saddle. He had a plan. He would grab ahold of the inside rein and pull that roan's head to him, then grab a big fistful of mane in the same hand, grab the saddle horn with his right hand, push his left knee into the saddle fender without putting a foot in the stirrup and hold on as that horse reared straight up and jumped away. As the horse was airborne, he'd swing into the saddle and off they went."

The blacksmith stopped talking as he heated the shoe in the forge and reshaped it with his rounding hammer.

"It took about a month for the horse to stop rearing and about three months of daily riding before that horse would walk on a loose rein."

The blacksmith pulled another shoe and trimmed the foot.

"One late snowy spring morning, Pa got on the horse and jumped a small creek with him. Well, I guess that roan horse wanted to show Pa he still had a little 'wild' in him, and when he landed on the other side of that creek, he came up a-buckin' and bucked a big perfect circle in the fresh snow. Pa lost a stirrup but stayed in the saddle. After that, that horse was plumb gentle. He was a one hell of good horse. Ol' Blue Mud was thirty when he died." The blacksmith smiled.

The blacksmith by this time had all the feet trimmed and the shoes shaped and started tacking them on. Creed swung the axe until he had all the wood split.

"Join us for dinner if you like," the man said.

"That is a nice offer, but I better keep moving. I'm starting to worry about snow on the pass," Creed replied.

"I don't know if you're riding to get away from anybody, but I saw three unsavory types in a pickup truck driving through here the other day. They looked like they were up to no good. Those guys weren't from around here and they looked like trouble."

Creed saddled the horses, packed the sorrel and thanked the blacksmith.

"Where you're headed, the country is going to get a lot greener—lots of grass, aspens, willows and pines. You'll cross the Snake River in the Swan Valley. There is an old barn after Victor that hunters will use for an overnight stay that might work for you. It's along the creek before you start up the pass. After that, the road goes over Teton Pass into the Hole. I've always pictured that heaven must look like that Jackson Hole country." The blacksmith stuck his hand out and shook Creed's. "Now, take care of yourself and be safe. Thanks for splitting the wood." He offered a warm smile.

"Thank you for shoeing my horses. We'll keep our eyes open for those men. Looking forward to the end of our journey," Creed replied.

***

Creed rode into sagebrush country again, but it had a different feel. The country was dry but did have more grass. Probably from the burn that Johnny had told him about. The charred stumps of big sagebrush were showing. The pleasant sound of meadowlarks would drift through the air as a few were darting here and there. The horses felt strong. He had been in the saddle for a few hours, and the sun had dropped into that late afternoon autumn warmth and glow. But he knew that this glorious day would soon disappear as the sun faded in the western sky. He rode up a slight hillside following a small creek and into a grassy pocket with a stand of aspens that were splashed with red and yellow leaves. Fall was showing its brilliant colors. His ears caught the sound of flush of birds. Three grouse flew into the trees, landing on branches. He tied the horses and then grabbed the rifle. He walked into the white aspen grove and with two shots had two grouse. He set the birds down with the rifle, unsaddled the horses and then picketed them in the thick grass so they could graze to their hearts' content. As he was setting up camp and building his fire, he felt the colder air descend as the sun was setting. His campsite gave him a broad view of the countryside. In the far distance, he would see a building or two and smoke coming from their chimneys.

As his fire was burning down to coals, he prepared a manny tarp for his blanket. A beautiful glow of muted pink lay on the horizon giving him a sense of euphoria. The first star of the evening twinkled overhead, and the cool air made its presence felt. He skinned the grouse then cut it up and dropped the meat into the frying pan that had a dollop of oil in it. As he stirred it, he heard the hoot of an owl and the barks from a pack of coyotes. Looking around, he couldn't spot any of them. He enjoyed his meal and looked at the darkening sky. He saw one shooting star and made a wish.

Creed checked on the horses one more time. They had eaten their fill of the good thick stand of grass. He tied them to two stout live aspens. Their coats were growing from the cooler night temperatures and the fading daily sunlight. Their bodies were getting ready for winter. Creed found them good. Cold and a few more early stars greeted him as he arranged his bedroll and turned in.

"Creed, Creed, honey, it's time to wake up. Come on, Creed. Rise and shine. The day's a-wastin'."

Creed was in that relaxed state somewhere between sleep and awake. He smiled as he heard his mother's voice, then he heard the engine. He jumped out of his bedroll, pulled on his boots and grabbed his jacket. He looked down the hill and saw a truck driving in the low sagebrush. He ran to his bedroll, grabbed everything for the panniers, stuffed them, saddled the horses and packed Jack and swung up. They could graze later, but right now he had to hightail it out of there. He rode to the edge and looked over. They were right below and driving towards him. Creed pulled Jack's head up close to him, wrapped and then tied the lead rope snug around Jack's neck and turned him loose. The horses sensed the tension as they took off across the hillside. They hit the sage at a high lope.

"Come on, boys, we just have to get into those hills and those pines." He leaned forward and urged the sorrel on.

The truck had stopped to let the men out to shoot and then started turning around.

Creed saw the first shot hit in front of him and veered to the right. Both horses were really running now. The men were working their lever action Winchesters and firing one after another. The bullets were hitting the soft ground and popping up puffs of dirt all around them. He heard a bullet whizzing by his head and then Jack tumbled to the ground, rolled and came up slightly dazed, but running again. The men got back in the truck and sped after the trio.

Creed pulled the sorrel to a stop, spun him around, waited as the truck approached and then fired two quick shots from his pistol. The first bullet went wide to the left, shattering the right headlight, but the second bullet did its damage as it tore through the thin radiator tin, causing a white cloud of hot steam. Creed holstered his gun as he wheeled the sorrel around and vanished as one into the timber.

The horses' sides were heaving and they were covered in a foamy lather when they finally came to a stop. Creed tied them to the trees and walked around Jack first. A bullet had grazed the top of his left hip. It was just a bloody surface wound and Creed thanked his lucky stars that Jack was fine. He would put some of Ohm's ointment on the wound once in camp. The sorrel was fine, but sweaty.

They rode through the timber where no truck could follow. After several hours of riding, he found a secluded clearing with a small creek and plenty of grass. They would stay here for the rest of the day and night. The town of Victor would be the last town before Jackson. This was the town to avoid because that was where all of the Spears gang would be waiting for him. The sky was a brilliant blue, any plant with a broad leaf had colors of yellow, red or orange on them, and the pines and firs were dark green against the blue.

After the run, the horses seemed tired. All the miles had added up. They were need of a good rest, but they still had the pass waiting for them. Creed picketed the horses and let them graze. He pulled his pistol from the holster, opened its gate and used the ejector rod to remove the two spent shells. He then pulled one cartridge at a time from his gun belt and reloaded his gun. He wanted to be ready for any more trouble, if it crossed his path. The pistol was only good at close range and the .22 was a last resort.

*Damn those Spears,* he thought. "They want it all," Creed said out loud as he stared at the horses.

The morning sky was an opaque blue with high thin clouds. The air had a chill and the horses had a sparkle in their eyes from the temperature. Creed broke camp and this day put the sawbuck on Jack again because of the light load. He put Om's ointment on Jack's wound.

He rode to the edge of the timber and looked down into the Swan Valley, watching the big river and the paved road. "Today we cross the Snake," he said aloud to the horses.

Creed and the horses worked their way down the hillside using the timber for cover. He needed daylight because of the terrain and the river. He could see the town of Victor from his location and wanted to avoid it and the Spears. He felt that Wyoming was near and would be safe.

As Creed rode, he heard a unique popping sound. It was something he had not heard before. He first looked in the trees and didn't see anything. Looking up, he saw a black raven flying on high in the blueness. It was making the noise as it enjoyed floating on the thermals.

A light snow was beginning to fall as he rode into the river bottom. In spots, the meadow grass rolled its green edge into the water adding to its beauty. As he approached the river's ford, he saw several large black trout dart for deeper water. The snow was being pushed by a light north wind, driving it into Creed's face. He had to tilt his hat into the wind to keep the snow out of his eyes. The horses' left sides had snow clinging to their coats. The horses splashed through the icy current to the other side. He trotted into the thick willows and headed for the hunter's barn. The low-slung log building came into view in the waning light.

The barn was near a creek that had a corral straddling the flowing water. It sat in front of a treed canyon directly south of it. It was far enough away from the road that it set Creed's mind at ease. There was good clean hay stacked inside. A reminisces of a warm campfire showed some hunter had left recently.

Creed unsaddled the horses, placed his gear in the opening of the barn, grained them and then turned them loose in the corral so they could get to water. The snow was getting heavier with big flakes coming straight down. The horses' backs were turning white. He moved his outfit into the barn and found stout pole-like structures stuck into the logs to place his saddles, blankets and panniers on. Next he caught up the horses and used the currycomb to remove the snow before he brought them into the barn. There were two large stalls that he tied them in. What was left of the moisture melted and dripped down their sides. Body heat was causing a very slight amount of steam to rise from them as their hides were drying out. Creed filled both feed bunks with hay.

There was a crudely made bench that he sat on in the barn as he ate some jerky for his dinner and stared at the falling snow. It was not worth the effort to make a fire. This was his last stop before Wyoming. He planned to leave at daybreak. He placed a manny tarp on a pile of hay and then his blanket. He drifted off into a restless sleep.

Creed woke to his coldest morning of the journey. He cautiously looked out of the opening of the barn. The snow had stopped during the night, covering the ground with about a foot of new powder, and the sky was clear. Creed bundled up and fed the horses their grain and more hay. He turned them loose into the corral so they could drink their fill of water. The sorrel got the pack today.

***

The morning sun was slow coming up since the mountains blocked it. Creed led the horses from the ground, walking them so he could warm up. He could see the road off to the north and a car every once in a while. The sun was glowing at the top of the pass. Soon he would be stepping into Wyoming.

He entered a small meadow that was surrounded by tall willows. He was between the two horses as they stopped, spooked slightly and stared into the willows in front of them. A gunshot rang out and both horses jumped. He looked ahead of him and there was Craw holding a pistol, pointing it in the air. His brother, Todd, was standing by his side. Both were in the mountain's shadow.

"Well, look who I have in my sights, the California fugitive trying to escape justice," he bellowed.

"Your idea of justice and mine don't even come close," Creed snapped back.

"Stay right there, or we'll shoot your horses and then you. You've been a real pain in my ass trying to catch up with you, Creed. I thought for sure we would have caught you in Susanville or Winnemucca. Don't know how you managed to get rid of Sheriff Johnson, but you did. Well, it ends here today, you God damned slippery bastard. Now that I have you in my sights, I want to let you in on a little secret. I was with Fred that night when he set your parents' house on fire. He was mad at your dad for reporting him to the brand inspector because of the two slick horses he had in his corral. He was just gonna scare your dad with the fire, but it burned too fast and the rest is history." Phil smiled wickedly.

"I always wondered about that fire. And the rest isn't history. You killed the two people I cared the most about. You and your family have all the money, livestock and land that anyone could have, but it's not enough. You're just a greedy, ruthless, worthless bastard with no soul," Creed spat.

"You never can have enough money because more money gives you more power and that's what's it all about. I don't need a soul." Phil laughed.

"I can't bring my folks back, but I want you to face justice. So, what are your plans, Phil? Are you taking me in, or will you just conveniently shoot me in the back?" Creed asked.

"You know, I rightly haven't decided. But I have a feeling the story will be 'he tried to escape and was killed in a shootout.'"

Creed was still standing between the horses as he grabbed hold of the saddle horn with his right hand and high up on the packsaddle's lash rope with his left as Craw was talking. The sorrel was on his left side and he nudged him with his left knee and whistled. The sorrel jumped out and the roan came along blocking Creed in the middle. Creed held on as they jumped out and did a running bounce as they ran in order to stay with them. They had gone about twenty feet when Creed let go, tucked and dropped to the ground. The horses ran on and then spun around to look at Creed and the men.

Phil fired a shot that clipped Creed's jacket as he fell to the snow. Creed was lying prone on the ground as he steadied his pistol with both hands and shot. The bullet hit Phil's left knee, making a *thud* sound, which spun him around, causing him to fall into the snow. Todd went for his gun as a loud shot rang out to Creed's left, hitting the ground in front of him.

Two men were horseback, pointing their rifle at the two Spears. A man in a black hat yelled at Todd, "Get rid of that gun, or the next shot will go right through you!"

Phil was on the ground, moaning in pain as he held his knee. Creed kept his gun pointed at Phil as Todd helped him stand.

"Creed, we're friends!" the man sitting on a buckskin horse in the sunshine yelled. "I'm U.S. Marshal Norman Hope out of Salt Lake. This here is Sheriff Jim Ferry out of Idaho Falls. Ben Ames is a friend, and he told me you were wrongly accused. Nora came out of her coma and told us everything. I'm here to take in what's left of the Spears gang. There's quite a laundry list of charges against the entire Spears family and their hired hands. They've been up to no good for a long time."

"So, you were the man looking for me in Twin Falls and Fort Hall?" Creed asked, still pointing his gun at Phil.

"Yep, I was trying to find you before these fellows did. I do apologize I was a little late. But I'm impressed how you handled yourself. If you ever want a job as a U.S. marshal, I'd be more than happy to pin the badge on you."

"Well, as far as I'm concerned, you were right on time. And I'll think about the job offer." Creed laughed with relief.

The marshal and sheriff rode over to the brothers. Todd was steadying his brother, Phil. The sheriff swung down from the black horse he was riding and picked up the Spears' guns.

"We are expecting a deputy coming this way in a bit so we can transport them to a jail in Idaho Falls. We caught a bunch of them yesterday while they were waiting for you in Victor," Norman said.

"Sure appreciate that, Marshal," Creed said as he holstered his pistol and walked over to Craw whose pant leg was soaked with blood. Creed could see he was in extreme pain.

Looking at Craw, Creed said, "I'll never forgive you for what you and your brother did to my parents. Never. But I just want you to know that I'm not like you. When I arrived at the Ameses, Fred was trying to rape Nora. He was enraged that I was there and tried to kill me. I tried to stop your brother several times before he fell on his knife. He alone is responsible for his death. Believe it or not."

Craw just stared at Creed. He knew he was caught, and he had to face the courts for all he had done. The bullet had clipped Phil's knee and bone fragments were showing.

"You had to try to have it all at any cost, but today's not your day, Phil. Today your cheating and conniving have caught up with you. You'll be lucky if the doctors can save that leg," Creed said in disgust.

"You son of a bitch!" Phil yelled at Creed as he tried to punch him in the face. Creed moved his head to the side as the punch flew by. Creed stood solid on the packed snow as he landed a punch squarely on Phil Spear's face, making a cracking sound. Creed's internal rage against this man was concentrated in the power of his fist. Phil dropped unconscious to the cold ground.

"Well, it will easier to take him this way." Sheriff Ferry grinned and spat out a plug of tobacco.

"You can go back to California an innocent man," Marshal Hope said.

"That's good to know, but I've come this far so I'll keep going to see my friend and this Jackson Hole country he's been telling me about. When I get settled, I'll write Ben and Nora a letter so you know where to get in touch with me. When you see them, please give them my best," Creed said.

"Creed, I will be pleased to do that. They are waiting to hear all about you," the marshal replied.

The sheriff was nodding in agreement and said, "Now just up the road a piece, you'll see a well used trail, used mostly by elk hunters this time of year. It'll take you up and over the pass to a little place in Wyoming called Wilson right on the edge of Jackson Hole."

"You can take off, Creed, and enjoy your freedom. We will take care of everything here." Norman smiled.

Creed caught up his horses. He walked over to Norman and Jim, shook their hands and said, "Thanks again for everything. Thanks for showing up when I needed you most."

***

The fall storms had laid down a good snow on top of the pass. The snow was up to the horses' chests, but it was a light, dry snow that gave easily as they walked through it.

Loaves of stack hay could be seen in the valley's meadows below. As Creed admired the view, the solid wing beats of a Clark's nutcracker could be heard in the still air as it flew by them. Starting down the trail, Creed met some hunters packing out their elk as they were descending into the valley. They had shot a cow elk and had quartered it. They were packing it out on two horses, front quarters on one packhorse and hindquarters on another. Creed was amazed at the amount of meat—each quarter was the size of a California deer. The hunters invited him to ride along with them to Wilson.

Once in Wilson, he got directions to the Snake River Ranch. The valley floor was almost free of snow as he crossed Fish Creek and headed north into the cottonwoods along the Snake River. On the edge of a large clearing stood the ranch's two-story log house. Near the front steps, there was a stout rail to tie his horses to. He walked up to the door and grabbed the big horseshoe doorknocker and gave it two solid whacks.

The door opened and it was Bud's wife, Suzie.

"My God, Creed, it's you!" She laughed, giving Creed a big hug. "You finally came to see us, and you came a horseback. Bud is going to be thrilled. He's down in the barn. Let me get my coat and we'll head over there."

They visited as they walked, Creed leading his tired horses. The log barn was long and filled with stalls for teams of workhorses. Suzie hollered for Bud at its entrance.

"Bud, you've got a visitor. You'll never guess who."

A tall man came out of one of the stalls, squinting as he stared into the sunlight. As he got closer, he saw it was Creed.

"Well, I'll be danged. You finally came to see God's country. Hey, it's great to see you," Bud said as they shook hands and he grabbed his friend's shoulder. "Rory was in touch and he told me about the Spears. Are they still a worry for you?" Bud asked.

Creed told them the U.S. marshal had caught up with them.

"My God, Creed. Thank God you made it. It is just great to have you here. I've been looking for a good man. You interested?" Bud asked.

"You know, I could use a job about now and three squares a day. Yep, that would be nice." Creed grinned.

"I've got a nice pasture we can turn your horses into where they will be unbothered by themselves," Bud offered.

"They'll love that."

"So, what are the names of these fine looking animals?" Bud asked as he stroked their necks and admired them.

"The roan is Jack, who Rory gave me. And you know... I never named the sorrel. I just called him Joe's horse. I guess I better give him a name after all these miles. I borrowed him from Joe in Quinsy. So I guess I'll call him Quinsy because that's where we came from. I could not have had two better horses then these." Creed smiled appreciatively as he rubbed their necks.

Creed had arrived in Jackson Hole ahead of the heavy winter snowstorms and cold north winds. Winter soon arrived, however, and Creed was busy feeding the cows with a big team down along the Snake River where the moose lived. He had a small cabin to stay in with a woodstove. He hung his gun on a hook by the door, just in case. After feeding in the mornings, he'd take turns riding his horses through the cowherd to do any doctoring in the afternoons. He was enjoying his free life with no worry of being pursued.

One snowy afternoon, Bud's wife arrived back from town with the mail as Creed and the other men were eating dinner in the cookhouse.

"Creed, I got all your letters mailed that you gave me, and you actually got two today." She smiled as she held them out.

"Thanks, Suzie," Creed said as reached for them.

The first envelope was from the University of Wyoming Law School and the other brought a big smile to his face. It had "Sweeney" on the return address.

Creed smiled and looked at Suzie as he opened the envelope.

"Well, I'll be. She wants to come up here and see me!"

The End

# About The Author

I cowboyed for a number of years on the Blackfeet Indian Reservation in northern Montana, Jackson Hole, Wyoming, and the Lemhi Valley of Idaho. I also was a hunting guide in the Gros Ventre Mountains of Wyoming. Rode horseback down the Continental Divide from Missoula, Montana to Jackson, Wyoming. Fought forest fires for the USFS and guided on the Snake River. And I know that doesn't mean anything if you aren't interested in my writing or stories. "Creed" is first my first novel, and I hope you enjoy it.

Made in the USA
Las Vegas, NV
19 August 2021

28482538R00062